GUARDIANS
OF THE FUTURE

Also by Max Mason

Super Secret Super Spies: Mystery of the All-Seeing Eye

SUPER SECRET SUPER SPIES

GUARDIANS OF THE FUTURE

MAX MASON

ILLUSTRATED BY
DOUGLAS HOLGATE

Quill Tree Books
An Imprint of HarperCollinsPublishers

Produced by Alloy Entertainment
30 Hudson Yards, New York, NY 10001
www.alloyentertainment.com

Library of Congress Control Number: 2022933120
ISBN 978-0-06-291572-6

Typography by Joel Tippie
22 23 24 25 26   PC/LSCH   10 9 8 7 6 5 4 3 2 1

First Edition

To all the real-life Dougs out there. Stay weird.

CHAPTER 1

La pazienza è la virtù dei forti.
Patience is a virtue of the strong.

It was hot for an October morning, and Maddie Robinson reluctantly rode her scooter to the single-story, large redbrick building that housed the Franklinville Middle School.

Maddie didn't dislike the sixth grade; it was just that her life outside of it was so much more exciting. Still, she trudged there day after day. That morning, like every other, Maddie kissed her cousin Jessica goodbye, yelled, "Later!" to Jessica's husband, Jay, and headed to school.

Beads of sweat pooled under the sweater Jessica had made for her. It was in Maddie's favorite color, too—neon green. Except for the part at the bottom, where Jessica had run out of neon-green yarn and finished it with orange.

Looks . . . weird, Maddie thought when Jessica first held it up. *Just the right amount of weird.*

After all, Maddie wasn't a regular kid. She led a double life. On the surface, she was a just another middle schooler who liked science, strawberry ice cream, and inventing things. She rode her scooter to and from school, did her homework, did her chores—all super-normal things.

But last year, Maddie had been recruited by a super secret organization called the Illuminati, to be trained as one of the world's youngest and most elite super spies. She'd gone on top secret missions, cracking codes and finding clues to some of history's biggest questions. And she'd even saved the world (not to brag, but it was kind of a big deal). During her first real mission, she'd transformed her science-fair project, the Electrical Enhancer, into an invention that provided the entire world with free energy! And she'd defeated the world's greatest inventor-turned-supervillain, Zander Lyon, in the process. Zander had disappeared into the Hudson River without a trace, leaving the Illuminati— and the rest of the world—a more peaceful place without his evil schemes.

Maddie wondered what her classmates would think of her if they knew she was the reason the world had free energy, or that she had outsmarted the famous Zander Lyon by solving mysterious clues and finding the Statue of Liberty when it disappeared. The only downside of being a super secret super spy, Maddie realized, was that she had to keep it super secret. Not even her cousin Jessica could know . . . or her parents, if she'd known where they were.

Since she couldn't share the truth about her secret identity, Maddie liked being just a teeny bit weird. So her mismatched sweater was perfect.

Dozens of other kids streamed around Maddie, racing up to the big front doors painted in the school's colors, blue and yellow. Maddie took a deep breath, locked up her scooter, and entered.

Maddie liked school well enough: she liked learning, she liked the science lab, and she even liked the cafeteria, even though the food was somehow always 25 percent wetter than it should be. But she didn't have her own group of friends here, like she did in her life as a super spy. For starters, it wasn't easy to make new friends when she was hiding an enormous, very important, super-secret secret.

And also, she didn't like the same things as the other kids at her school. She had no real opinion about Chase Chance's latest music video, or why the fall musical would be *Cats*—again (the choral director, Ms. Tiverton, was obsessed)—or even whether gross Mr. Fullerton, whose false teeth were always falling out of his mouth, would finally retire. She'd much rather be lost in thought with an idea for a new invention, like how to attach a new feature to her tricked-out hyper-phone (which was short for HYbrid Personalized Enhanced Reconstructible phone), a replacement for the one that she'd lost in the Hudson River at the end of her first mission.

Besides, she had friends. They were just all super spies, like her. She wondered what Lexi, Caleb, Sefu, and Doug were up to right now. She hadn't seen them since their last mission several weeks ago, rescuing a man in Florida who had floated into the middle of the ocean in an inner tube and accidentally discovered a secret underwater Illuminati research lab.

Lexi was in another state, Caleb traveled a lot with his jet-setting parents, and Sefu was in Egypt during the school year. The only one close by was Doug, but he attended a private school on the other side of the city, and his parents signed him up for so many activities (accordion lessons, soccer, pottery class, tap dancing) in the hopes of helping him make friends that he didn't have any time to actually *see* his friend Maddie. Though they'd all kept in touch with old-fashioned letters written in a secret code, Maddie wished she could hang out with the four of them in person again. Until her next mission, though, she'd just have to wait.

After a quick trip to her locker, Maddie jogged to the classroom for her first-period history class and slid into a desk in the front row.

Mr. Onderdonk took attendance, and then Emily, who always volunteered for everything, passed out textbooks with an air of importance.

"Good morning, students!" said Mr. Onderdonk.

"Good morning!" the class answered—mostly enthusiastic, peppered with a few yawns and one loud burp. Probably Johnny, who was always burping, which somehow made him *more* popular, rather than less.

Maddie pulled out her notebook and pencil, ready to take notes. She had exactly fourteen pencils with her that day (nine in her backpack, two in her pockets, one behind each ear, and one in her hand), and she worried that maybe that wasn't enough. Her father had always told her to have something handy to write down her ideas before she forgot them. And her mother had had several pencils at hand all the time, poking through the messy bun she always wore.

Maddie sighed, feeling a familiar heaviness in her chest. She missed them. She missed their advice, their encouragement, their hugs. Maddie couldn't believe that it had been almost three years since her parents went missing on a scientific expedition to the North Pole, meaning that Maddie had to go live with her cousins. Most people had assumed the worst—even the company her parents had worked for sent a sympathy fruit basket—but a small part of Maddie still held out hope. She wished more than anything that they could've been the ones to kiss her goodbye that morning.

That was why Maddie always carried extra pencils. And why she wanted to learn everything she could in school, and outside of it—so that maybe someday she could use her knowledge and her Illuminati connections to figure out what had really happened to her family.

"This semester," Mr. Onderdonk started, "we're going to study one of the most important, fascinating, and unusual historical figures. Someone who made a huge impact in art, but also in science. A painter. A visionary. An inventor."

Maddie's ears pricked up at "inventor."

"Any guesses?" Mr. Onderdonk asked, bouncing on his heels.

"Bill—*burp*—Gates?" Johnny asked.

"Historical, I said! This is history class," Mr. Onderdonk said.

"Marie Curie?" Emily said.

"Good guess—but she's far too recent. Think back farther."

"Benjamin Franklin?" Maddie blurted out, forgetting to raise her hand. She knew he was an inventor, and on her first mission, she'd been up close and personal with some of his ideas.

"Another good guess, but I'm talking fifteenth century here. We are doing an entire unit on"—Mr. Onderdonk made a grand gesture with his hands, as if he were opening a portal to a vast cavern of knowledge—"Leonardo da Vinci!"

"I know him!" said Johnny. "He's one of those turtles that knows karate!"

"Wrong," said Mr. Onderdonk. "The artist. The visionary. The original Renaissance man."

"The guy who painted the *Mona Lisa*?" Maddie said, remembering the refrigerator magnet in Jessica and Jay's apartment, with the mysterious lady with a smirky smile and murky background.

"Yes! And that's not all he did. He was a multidisciplinary legend!" Mr. Onderdonk's eyes shone with excitement. "Get out your pencils and take notes!"

Maddie got out another pencil. Now she was holding *two* pencils, poised over her notebook, which was totally covered in design doodles for a noise-canceling earpiece that would automatically tune out Johnny's burps. *Too bad I can't do anything about the smell*, she thought.

"Many call da Vinci a genius, a unique talent with an insatiable curiosity about so many areas of study: art, botany, anatomy, architecture, and weather. He left behind notebooks filled with his ideas, but we don't know the full extent of his genius, as many of his notebooks were lost." Mr. Onderdonk clicked on the projector, which splashed diagrams of geometric shapes, people, and even a mechanical lion all over the whiteboard. "Da Vinci was interested in both science and art. He designed and built things that were way ahead of his time."

Maddie found herself captivated by one of the scientific diagrams on the whiteboard. It looked like some kind of flying machine, a frame supporting two winglike shapes. It was drawn from several angles, so that each component was visible, and it was similar in style to the plans Maddie

created on her tablet when she was working on a new
design. It reminded her of how she always wanted to know
how things worked, whether it was an airplane or a microwave or a particle accelerator. She also wanted to know
what *could* be possible, even if it hadn't been invented yet.
And da Vinci seemed to be asking those same questions,
five hundred years ago. She'd had no idea Leonardo da

Vinci wasn't just another famous painter—he'd invented things, like she did!

"Your assignment, should you choose to accept it—and you *must* accept it, since it's half your grade for the semester"—Mr. Onderdonk chuckled at his own joke—"is to complete a research project on Leonardo da Vinci, focusing on one work of art or an invention that demonstrates the concept of *innovation* and how that innovation has impacted the world. You can pick anything you want, as long as it was created or designed by da Vinci, and you will share your research with the entire school at the end of the semester in a multimedia presentation."

At that, the class groaned. The pressure was on. Maddie didn't love speaking in front of crowds, but she *did* like the sound of this assignment. She couldn't wait to start! The only hard part would be figuring out which invention to focus on.

Maddie wished she could ask da Vinci a thousand questions: Where did he get his ideas? Did he ever fail, or did he succeed at everything he tried? Did he know people would call him a genius? Or did people think he was weird, like they did Maddie?

The bell rang and the class filed out into the hallway. Maddie couldn't stop thinking about the project. After four classes and what seemed like hours (well, it actually *had* been hours), it was finally lunchtime. Maddie thought about skipping lunch and sneaking off to the library to find out more about da Vinci's inventions and narrow down her search for a research topic. But she could smell something cheesy—it was Pizza Day in the cafeteria. She tossed her backpack into her locker and sprinted to the lunchroom, so she could be at the front of the lunch line. She could research da Vinci online on her phone while she ate.

It was hard to be a visionary genius on an empty stomach.

CHAPTER 2

Non rimandare a domani quello che puoi fare oggi.
Don't put off tomorrow what you can do today.

Holding her tray bearing a less-than-sizzling, ultra-greasy slice of pizza, Maddie scanned the cafeteria, looking for a seat. Tables were filling up quickly, and it looked like people were saving seats for each other by draping sweatshirts over empty chairs. Maddie heard a burp, followed by peals of laughter. Johnny's table was full. She looked for Emily—she was nice even if she was a know-it-all—but Emily's table was swarmed with her musical-theater friends, who were practicing *Cats*. One girl was actually pouring her mini-carton of milk onto a plate and lapping it up like a cat.

Really committing to the character. Maddie had to give her that.

Maddie spotted an empty seat at the teachers' table,

where the ones who had lunchroom duty sat and sipped coffee and chatted about which reality TV stars they would most like to meet in real life. Ms. Tiverton noticed Maddie and waved her over. Maddie knew she wasn't the choral director's favorite—Maddie could *not* carry a tune—but she appreciated the invitation to sit, even if it was at the teachers' table. She plopped down next to Ms. Tiverton.

"*Soooooo*, Maddie," said Ms. Tiverton in a *faaaancy* voice Maddie considered necessary for *aaaactors*, "how in touch are you with your feline side?"

"I'm, uh, more of a dog person, I guess," said Maddie.

"Hmm, *perhaaaaps* we could create a canine role for you in the fall musical, then," Ms. Tiverton said. "I'm sure you could use an activity to take your mind off . . . you know."

And there it was. Maddie gazed up in pain at the sympathetic look Ms. T. was giving her. Maddie hated those looks. She had gotten them from every single adult ever since her parents disappeared. She knew they meant well, but it just made her feel worse. She wished they'd stop giving her looks and say what they meant: since you became an *orphan*.

Maddie eyed her gloopy-looking slice of pizza, but before she could bite into it, her Illuminati-issued S.M.A.R.T.W.A.T.C.H. buzzed. A message popped up on its display: MISSION INCOMING. REPORT TO THE NEAREST ILLUMINATI COMMAND CENTER IMMEDIATELY. "Yes!" shouted Maddie, way too loudly. She looked up at the startled Ms. Tiverton. "I, um, just hit my step count for the day," she said. "Excuse me!"

Maddie dropped her pizza and ran out of the room toward the nearest Illuminati Command Center. Thankfully, she didn't have to go far.

Maddie stopped in the hall at the janitor's closest. She looked around before knocking softly. "Mr. Sneely?" she whispered. A few moments later, an old man in a gray-green uniform opened the door.

"Oh, hello, Maddie," said Mr. Sneely.

"Sorry to bug you, Mr. S.," said Maddie. "But I just walked past the science lab and there appeared to be some sort of situation involving Mr. Fullerton's toupee and a Bunsen burner."

"Not again!" said Mr. Sneely. He grabbed his mop and ran out as quickly as he could, which was extremely slowly.

Maddie looked around once more to make sure the coast was clear, then stepped into Mr. Sneely's closet and closed the door. She didn't bother to flick on the light. "Identification: Maddie Robinson," she said into the darkness.

"Authentication code?" a robotic voice said.

"*Cognitio. Virtus. Imperium,*" said Maddie. Suddenly, a set of hidden LED lights turned on, giving the room a soft, golden glow. The three walls of the closet spun around, hiding Mr. Sneely's cleaning gear and revealing a futuristic array of gadgets, info screens, and even a flight control deck to pilot the fleet of drones Maddie had stashed on the school's roof.

Maddie felt like she had waited forever for a chance to go back into the field. "I wonder where they'll send me," she whispered with glee. She started to pull up her mission briefing on one of the screens. *Dubai? The Bermuda Triangle? Outer space?!*

A holographic globe appeared and began to zoom in on the location of Maddie's next mission. "Okay, it's in the US," she said as the globe continued to zoom in. "Oh . . . it's right here in Philly!" The globe zoomed in again to its final location. "My next mission is in . . . my school loading zone? Huh?"

Maddie was confused, but she didn't hesitate. She rushed down the hall, grabbed her backpack from her locker, and headed in the direction of the entrance. She pushed open the heavy door to the outside and found herself just a few steps away from the driveway lined in orange cones, where adults dropped off their kids in the morning.

A familiar light blue minivan sat idling, waiting for her. Maddie noticed tons of bumper stickers, and a discreet golden triangle was the hood ornament. She smiled. She knew what that meant.

The minivan door slid open, revealing the comfy leather seats in its air-conditioned depths. Maddie hopped inside. *Weird*, she thought. She couldn't see the back of the van— there was a mirrored panel behind the first row of seats. *Must be a security panel to keep bad guys locked up in the back.* She checked out her reflection.

She noticed that bunches of hair had escaped the braid that Jessica had done for her this morning, and that she had a stain—jalapeño cream cheese, she suspected—right on the front of her sweater. Ugh.

Suddenly, the mirrored panel slid down to reveal three smiling faces. "SURPRISE!!!!" the faces shouted, and the minivan closed its door and drove itself off school property and onto a quiet side street. "Lexi! Caleb! Doug!" Maddie screamed, and they all tackled her in a big hug. "Where's Sefu?" she asked.

"Sefu's running point at HQ," said Caleb, adjusting his glasses. Those were new, since last time Maddie had seen him.

"But he's on speaker!" Lexi said.

"Hello, Maddie!" Sefu's voice boomed out of the mini-van speakers. The van was picking up speed.

"How is everybody? I missed you all so much!" Maddie said.

"There will be time for catchup later," Sefu's voice said,

as his face appeared, hovering, above one of the car's holographic info panels. "We have a—"

"We have a mission!" Doug cried, bouncing lightly on his seat.

Sefu sighed. "Doug, if you could please let me do my job?"

"Sorry," Doug said. He drummed his hands on his armrest. "A mission!" he squeaked.

"SHHHHH!!!!" everyone said.

"Sorry again," Doug said. "A mission," he whispered to himself with a smile.

Maddie couldn't help but smile a little bit too. She was finally back with her friends, doing what she loved: saving the world, one mission at a time.

CHAPTER 3

L'unione fa la forza.
Unity is strength.

"As I was saying—" Suddenly the minivan lurched upward, and Maddie's stomach dropped as they rose up into the sky.

"AAAHH!" Caleb yelled, fumbling for his seat belt, which was already fastened securely across his chest.

"WOO!" Lexi yelled, pumping her first so hard that her spiky blue hair (with new purple highlights) trembled.

Maddie had forgotten how being in an Illuminati-designed flying car felt like riding a roller coaster sometimes. As the minivan swooped up and over houses and trees and buildings, she was glad she hadn't eaten her soggy cafeteria pizza.

"We're taking you to a concert venue eighty miles north of the city," Sefu continued.

"A concert?" said Caleb. "That doesn't sound urgent."

"It sounds fun," said Lexi.

Sefu's voice boomed from the speakers. "It's Chase Chance, and—"

"Chase Chance!" Lexi cried. "THE Chase Chance? I looooove his songs!"

"I prefer classical music," said Caleb. "Though his dance moves are pretty good. If you're into that sort of thing."

"Focus, agents!" Sefu shouted just as the flying minivan made a loud whooshing noise, doubling its speed. The kids were pressed back into their leather seats as they zoomed over the outer suburbs of Philadelphia.

"Chase is doing a huge benefit concert for a hospital out there tonight. The crowd is already there. Thousands of people, kids and families. But a freak tornado has just formed a few miles away, and the amphitheater is in its path!"

"Shouldn't all those kids be in, you know, school right now?" asked Maddie.

"Are you kidding?" said Lexi. "My mom took me out of school to see Chase last year! She wanted to go as badly as I did."

"The tornado is picking up speed as we speak," said Sefu.

"Sounds serious," Caleb said. "Unlike Chase's music."

"It *is* serious—that's why we're rushing you to the scene. You need to stop a tragedy from happening. Get the people out of the way of the tornado, or get the tornado away from the people. And protect Chase Chance at all costs!"

Now the minivan was whizzing faster, over the farms and fields. Maddie peered out the window and noticed the brilliantly clear blue sky, with no sign of a storm in sight. *Not exactly tornado weather,* she thought.

"A tornado?" she said. "Are you sure? This is Pennsylvania!"

"Yes," said Sefu. "According to the historical data, this one is five times bigger than any tornado seen in this area before—and it just sprang up out of nowhere!"

"Send us the coordinates and all relevant data," Caleb said, whipping out a device that looked like a detective's pad and pen with a holographic screen floating on top of it.

"Extreme weather can really wreak havoc on cucumber farms," said Lexi. Maddie grinned. Lexi's family operated a cucumber farm, so she knew all about them.

"Do you have anything on radar and atmospheric pressure?" Lexi asked, pulling up a weather-tracking radar screen on one of the other digital panels. A red-and-blue diagram of a tornado filled the screen. "Apparently, some sort of weather anomaly caused a bunch of warm, humid air to run smack into cold air, creating this freak tornado!"

"Sefu, we'll need schematics for the amphitheater, the

parking lot, and all surrounding structures," Caleb said as he took notes on his device. "We've got to figure out how to get all those people to safety!"

"What should I do?" Doug yelled frantically, looking from Lexi, to Caleb, and then to Maddie.

"You keep cool," Sefu said over the speakers. "Think of something to say to all the scared kids when we get closer. I'll deploy the external megaphone. You need to keep those kids calm and make sure they follow our directions."

"GOT IT!" screamed Doug nervously. "I mean, got . . . it . . . ," he said with an exaggerated calm, deep voice.

Maddie pulled up the Illuminati research portal on her hyper-phone and searched for ways to stop a tornado. She frowned as she read down the list. "We could drop a nuclear bomb into it—uh, *no*. Building a giant wall or dome around the area—not enough time for that. Wait a minute. . . ." Maddie's finger hovered over a link entitled *Microwaves*.

She cringed as she remembered the time she'd hooked up her cousin's microwave oven to an early prototype of her Electrical Enhancer and accidentally caused the entire Philadelphia metro region to lose power. But through that mistake, she'd learned a lot about microwaves. She knew they caused water molecules to vibrate, which was what heated up chicken nuggets or frozen pizza bagels quickly.

Maddie looked at the red-and-blue diagram of the tornado. It was caused by the different temperatures and humidity of air systems. But what if she eliminated that temperature difference? If she could heat up the cooler air, would that slow—or stop—the tornado? *Sure, it's TECHNICALLY possible*, she thought, *but could it actually work?*

She did some quick calculations.

"Sefu," Maddie said, "beam me the specs on the tornado's size, speed, and rate of spin. Please!"

She scribbled more notes on her screen. If they could aim microwaves into the heart of the tornado, it would dissipate. Maddie quickly explained her idea to the team.

"A classic 'Maddie idea,'" Caleb said. "Extremely brilliant and possibly impossible. I like it."

"Maddie to the rescue!" Lexi said, pumping her fist into the air.

The group worked together to craft a plan, dividing up who would handle what.

As the minivan began its descent, Maddie glanced out the window again and saw that the pretty blue sky had turned a sickly greenish color. They flew toward the concert venue, which was surrounded by an endless parking lot filled with cars baking in the haze of the green sky. Maddie worried about what would happen if the tornado reached that parking lot. Cars and SUVs weighing several tons could be extremely dangerous if they got picked up by the intense winds. As they got closer, they could see a big stage and covered pavilion with rows and rows of seats, and a grassy field filled with people slowly panicking. The green sky dimmed as heavy clouds scudded past, and the wind whipped the multicolored flags marking the entrances to the amphitheater so hard that it looked like the flagpoles might snap.

"YIKES!" screamed Doug. "Over there!"

He pointed out the window as the minivan came to a slightly bumpy landing. About a mile or two away, they could see a giant black column of whirling wind and dust, churning up a cloud of debris at its base. "So, um, Illuminati agents aren't allowed to get scared, right?" asked Doug. "'Cause, I mean, I'm totally not," he added unconvincingly.

Caleb's face was grim. Lexi whispered something under her breath. Maddie was scared, too, but she knew they all had to be brave. Thousands of kids were counting on them!

The tornado picked up speed, creating a path of destruction as it plowed through a nearby tree line, snapping massive oaks as if they were toothpicks and filling the air with branches and leaves. It was heading right for the super spies and thousands of innocent kids and adults. The sky darkened to an even weirder greenish-gray, and the wind roared like a freight train.

Maddie trembled. The force of the tornado was so powerful—she could see stop signs and bales of hay, trash, and even some rocks being carried violently through the air by the howling wind.

"Okay, we can do this!" she said to her team with more confidence than she felt. "Everyone clear on the plan?"

"Yes!" her teammates replied in unison.

They popped in wireless earpieces, jumped out of the van, and split up. The wind was intense, and raindrops began to sting like needles as they fell.

Caleb and Doug raced toward a group of kids in the

parking lot who were dangerously close to the twister, ready to wrangle them to safety.

Lexi yelled something to Maddie, but even with their earpieces, the wind tore the words away and Maddie had no idea what she'd said.

"We need to get closer!" Maddie yelled. She and Lexi tried to walk into the wind, but the force was so strong, they could barely step forward.

"I have a vehicular upgrade you might like," said Sefu into Maddie's earpiece. Suddenly, the minivan's back door popped off its hinges. Before it could hit the ground, four blue-white thrusters in the corners ignited, letting the door float six inches in the air.

"I believe we have a hoverboard!" said Maddie. She and Lexi jumped aboard. Using her body weight, Maddie tilted the floating panel forward. The makeshift hoverboard inched ahead at first, then took off like a rocket. "Hold on!" she yelled as they raced toward the column of wind and fury barreling down on them.

"We're leading the kids into the underground maintenance tunnels!" Caleb's voice crackled in Maddie's earpiece. "Hurry!"

The tornado towered above them like an angry skyscraper. Lexi tugged on Maddie's arm. They'd reached a wooden utility pole in one of the fields, and they hopped off the hoverboard. Maddie quickly took out her hyper-phone and pressed the buttons activating the Electrical Enhancer function. She had it turned all the way to maximum strength, sucking up half the power from all electronic devices in a twenty-mile range.

Meanwhile, Lexi pulled out an Illuminati-issued Swiss Army knife made of superstrong and supersharp metal alloys. She cut into the side of the utility pole, creating a deep crack in the wood. Then she pushed gently on the pole, yelled "Timber!" and ran around to the other side. With her strong muscles, built from playing practically every sport and wrestling with her eight brothers, Lexi carefully lifted the heavy utility pole until it was pointed in the direction of the tornado.

"A few more feet to the right!" Maddie yelled, and Lexi's arms strained, rotating the pole so that it pointed exactly at the tornado. Sweat beaded on Lexi's face, but she gritted her teeth and remained strong, holding the pole in position as the wind blew harder.

I really hope this works, she thought desperately. Maddie realized just how powerful the twister was as it uprooted trees and boulders—and it was nearly upon them! She pressed the last button, sending an invisible beam of microwaves from her phone to the metal transformer on the top of the utility pole.

A blinding light, a shower of sparks, and a weird humming sound emanated from the utility pole.

Working together, Maddie and Lexi wrestled the tornado, targeting the microwave rays right to its core. Maddie increased the intensity of the microwave beam. The tornado plowed up plumes of soil, coating Maddie and Lexi with a layer of dirt. The power on Maddie's device was rapidly draining, even with the Electrical Enhancer, and she wondered with horror if her calculations had been too low.

"My arms!" Lexi yelled. "I can't hold it much longer!"

Just as Maddie feared her calculations had been wildly off, a billboard with Chase Chance's face on it ripped from its frame and flipped end over end toward the young agents. They screamed as the billboard flew over their heads, and Maddie sent out a final burst of power from her device as her phone died. Suddenly, the tornado faltered, losing power as it spun slower and slower. Branches and rock fell to the ground until the twister dissipated into nothing more than a breeze.

They'd done it! She and Lexi stopped the tornado, just in time.

Lexi let the utility pole drop with a thud. She and Maddie sank to the ground, weak and weary. They were out of breath and covered with dirt, but they were *alive*.

The two girls laughed and helped brush mud from each other's faces.

"My radar is showing that tornado has disappeared," Sefu said through Maddie's earpiece. "Agents, are you okay?"

"We're okay," Maddie said, grinning. "We did it!" She heard whoops and cheers from her friends in her earpiece.

Just then, a mountain of a man in a neon tracksuit and wraparound sunglasses appeared. Maddie quickly put away her hyper-phone. Illuminati tech was strictly top secret, after all.

"Follow me," the man said, cracking his knuckles. Maddie looked at Lexi and gulped. It didn't seem like they had a choice. "Chase Chance would like a word."

CHAPTER 4

Tutto fumo e niente arrosto
All bark and no bite

The neon-clad, muscle-bound man led Lexi and Maddie to the parking lot, where Caleb and Doug waited. Everyone was wind-whipped and exhausted, but they were safe. The man silently led them to the arena, to a door marked with a sign that read *VIP ENTRANCE.*

Despite the fact that Maddie didn't even *like* Chase's music, she was still a little nervous. She had never met a pop star before. And she had no idea what this one wanted.

They entered a large room, and the first thing they saw was Chase Chance sprawled on a white couch, in full-on bad-boy-pop-star glory. He wore a jumpsuit in banana yellow, embellished with rhinestones and studs, with his

initials embroidered on every inch. His banana-yellow sneakers, looking brand-new and also embroidered with his initials, were casually propped up on the couch. Chase's hair was styled in his trademark messy swoop, which half hid his eyes and flared out behind his neck like a fluffy duck's tail. He looked up from his phone, and when he finally noticed the four Illuminati agents waiting just inside the door of the suite, a huge, lopsided grin transformed his face from utter boredom to unabashed joy.

At the sight of his smile, Lexi swayed, leaning hard against Maddie's shoulder. "Oh my gosh," Lexi whispered. Maddie had to admit, the smile was breathtaking. It was dazzling. It reminded her of a video she'd once seen online of golden retriever puppies eating a dish of ice cream.

"Y'all, I can't thank you enough!" Chase said, jumping to his feet. "You saved the tour—I mean, so many lives! You are true heroes." He bounded toward the four of them, offering his hand for an enthusiastic high five. Doug leaped up and smacked Chase's hand, and Chase went down the line.

Chase turned to address the rest of the people in the suite. "Hey, y'all, I want you to meet my best friends in the world!" He introduced the team to his manager, Shonda— and then to his voice coach, his assistant voice coach, his assistant, his other assistant, his assistants' two assistants, his life coach, his stylist, his hairdresser, his makeup artist, his masseuse, his choreographer, his agent, three lawyers, a butler, a photographer, and his "angles consultant."

"What's an angles consultant?" Maddie asked politely.

"Oh, she tells me which angle to hold my head in selfies, things like that. Her services cost a fortune, but it's totally worth it!" Chase said, as though it was obvious. "Let's all give these heroes a round of applause!" Chase's entourage obediently clapped—until he made a quick zip-it motion with his hand and they obediently stopped.

The butler, assisted by his assistant and Chase's

assistant's assistant, quickly handed out cups filled with a bright green liquid. Maddie sniffed it dubiously. It smelled fresh, and weirdly familiar.

"Ooh, it's cucumber soda!" squealed Lexi.

"Yeah, it's my favorite." Chase shrugged. "My color consultant said I should eat only green foods this week. Cucumber, spinach, green M&M's, that kind of thing."

"I . . . love . . . cucumber!" Lexi managed to sputter. Maddie strongly suspected she wanted to say *I love YOU* to Chase, and she stifled a giggle.

Chase led his entourage in a toast. "To the fearless team that saved many lives today, and prevented many lawsuits!"

"Hooray!" yelled the entourage.

"Hear! Hear!" yelled the lawyers. The suite filled with the clinking of glasses and laughter.

Maddie guzzled her cucumber soda. It really wasn't that bad.

"Fam, I need the room," Chase said. Abruptly, the laughter and chitchat stopped, and the entourage hustled out a side door.

Chase motioned the agents over to the pristine white couch. Maddie noticed she was still covered in dirt from the tornado. She didn't want to sit on the nice couch. Doug plopped right down, bouncing gently on the fluffy cushions. Caleb, Lexi, and Maddie remained standing awkwardly.

"Team," he said, looking at each of them. "You all are

the GOAT. All I do is sing. And dance. And write hit songs. And inspire millions. But you're out here saving lives!" Chase put his hand over his heart.

"Why are we goats?" Doug whispered.

"Greatest of all time, little dude," Chase said, pressing his palms together, with a serious expression on his face. "I wanted to thank you privately. As a pretty spectacular fourteen-year-old myself, I can tell you're not just regular kids. . . ."

Maddie glanced nervously at Caleb.

"I know who you really are."

Maddie gulped.

"Because I'm one of you!" Chase cried, his megawatt grin shining even brighter. He pulled aside the collar of his jumpsuit to reveal a delicate chain, hidden under his other necklaces, with a small gold triangle charm dangling from it. "Just call me: a super secret superSTAR!"

Doug's eyes grew huge. "You're Illuminati, too?" he gasped.

"Shh!" said Caleb.

Maddie coughed loudly, trying to cover up what Doug had said. After all, you couldn't be part of an ancient secret organization and spill the beans so easily. This could be a trap. Lexi continued to stare at Chase with a dreamy smile on her face.

"It's okay, y'all, see?" Chase whipped out his Illuminati-issued ID card. It looked just like a regular school ID, but instead of regular numbers and letters, it said: *ZBWLYZAHY KPCPZPVU.*

"Superstar Division," Caleb said, squinting at the letters. "Simple, really, just a rotation-seven cipher."

Maddie smiled. Caleb's talent of solving puzzles quickly sure came in handy. Chase whipped the ID card back into his wallet, which was overflowing with fifty-dollar bills and what looked like arcade tickets. Some of the coupons spilled out, and Doug handed them back to Chase.

"Thanks, man. I can't lose a single one of these. I'm saving up for a giant teddy bear."

Doug eyed the wads of cash peeking out of Chase's wallet.

"Can't he just buy one?" Caleb whispered to Maddie.

"Superstar Division, huh?" Maddie said. "Never heard of it."

"Oh yeah," Chase said. "We have agents in every genre of music. A bunch of Hollywood actors, too. And you know . . . my ex-girlfriend Sabrina," he whispered. "Totally Illuminati. Oops! Wasn't supposed to say that!

"We don't do cool missions like you guys. We just perform and try to sneak secret codes into our lyrics and our social media posts," Chase said.

"So, what level of clearance are you?" asked Caleb, adjusting his glasses.

"The highest! Level Three," Chase said, swooping back his hair.

Caleb looked at Maddie, who looked at Lexi, who looked

at Doug. They were all Level Ten. With a wordless look between them, they silently agreed not to tell Chase about the other levels.

"Anyway, I wanted to give you a little token of my appreciation for saving those fans, and me, and the tour," he said, handing out hoodie sweatshirts with his face emblazoned on the front—and back. "There's a download code for my newest album in the pocket," he said.

"Awesome!" said Doug, high-fiving Chase.

"Wow," said Caleb, looking at the sweatshirt dubiously. "I don't know what to say."

Maddie stared off into space, lost in thought.

"Thank you!" said Lexi, immediately pulling hers on. She elbowed Maddie, hissing in her ear, "Say thank you!"

"Sorry," Maddie said. "Thanks. I'm just still thinking about that tornado. It came out of nowhere! It doesn't make any sense."

Chase threw his arm around Maddie. "Hey, now. You saved the day, and that's all that counts! And anyway, weird things are always happening around me. Today it was the tornado. Yesterday, a sinkhole opened up right in front of my tour bus! We're soooo lucky we didn't fall in. And a few days ago, we were mobbed by this huge flock of birds during sound check. We had to cancel the show—a pelican bit through our wires and all our speakers were covered with, you know, bird poop. It was freaky."

Maddie leaned into the hug, but her mind was spinning.

A tornado, a sinkhole, and bewildering bird behavior—all happening to Chase Chance, all in the same week. She felt an odd sensation, a prickling at the back of her neck. It had to be more than a coincidence. Something very weird was happening around Chase. She knew the Illuminati did what they could, but bad people and bad things still came out of nowhere. Maddie wished she could find out who— or what—was coming after Chase before something truly terrible happened. After all, he seemed like a nice guy. Too bad there was no way to predict the future. . . .

Little did Maddie know, maybe there was.

CHAPTER 5

In bocca al lupo!
To be in the wolf's mouth

The team spent some time in Chase's suite, and Lexi and Doug were in awe. Maddie also gave herself a moment to marvel at Chase's greenroom. In addition to the huge white couch, there was a pinball machine (themed after Chase, naturally), two dozen electric guitars (Chase told fans he was learning how to play but hadn't found the right guitar yet), and even a full-size trampoline (with Chase's face painted at the exact center).

"The center is the sweet spot," said Chase, noticing where Maddie was looking. "That's where you get the highest jumps."

"Is it safe indoors?" asked Maddie. "Won't you hit your head on the ceiling?"

"Oh, definitely," said Chase. "But a little head injury every now and then is a small price to pay to feel like you're flying."

Just then, the spies' S.M.A.R.T.W.A.T.C.H.es beeped with a communiqué from Volkov, the Grand Sentinel of the Illuminati, aka their extremely intimidating leader: WELL DONE. MISSION COMPLETE. REPORT IMMEDIATELY TO CAMP MINERVA.

"Ahhhhhhhh!" Doug shouted at the top of his lungs. "Camp Minerva! It's real!"

"Of course it's real," said Lexi. "That's where we did our training last summer."

"It's the Illuminati's worldwide headquarters," added Maddie.

"I know," said Doug. "But I've never been there!"

Doug had been a major superfan of the Illuminati before he became an agent (and it seemed like he knew everything about it), but Maddie sometimes forgot he'd completely missed training. They'd actually met Doug on their first mission, looking for a secret Illuminati bunker where Doug was hiding, along with Benjamin Franklin's super secret inventions.

Caleb smiled. "Trust me, you're going to like it," he said.

Doug was practically hopping up and down. "I've heard they have the world's biggest library of secret knowledge—"

"True," said Maddie.

"—and a full skate park to test out flying Illuminati-issued skateboards—"

"That, um, might be true," said Lexi, unsure.

"—and they serve pills that let you grow ten feet tall so you can finally dunk a basketball!"

"That's definitely not true," said Caleb. "But if anyone is working on ten-foot growth pills, they're doing it at Camp Minerva."

The spies told Chase to break a leg at his next concert, then hopped into the minivan and were whisked up over the clouds, tinted pink in the fading sunlight. What felt like moments later, the sliding doors opened, revealing a white sand beach and aquamarine waves. Maddie shaded her eyes from the dazzling sun as a warm tropical breeze caressed her face. "We're here!" she said, brimming with excitement. She was still wearing her sweater, which was now covered in mud and drenched in sweat. Despite the heat, she didn't consider taking it off. She liked being a little bit weird, even on the island that was home to the world's true, ultrasecret center of power.

Maddie could see a huge glass tower topped by a giant golden globe peeking over the palm trees and felt a flutter of excitement.

"The Obelisk!" Doug whispered in awe.

"Yep," said Maddie. She smiled, proud that she was part of such an advanced secret society dedicated to keeping the world safe. "It's got dozens of floors full of researchers and scientists. And philosophers and futurists and poets and all kinds of way-out thinkers, too."

"Cool," said Doug. "But not nearly as cool as being a field agent, like us."

Maddie laughed. "Hey! Science *is* cool!" she said before adding, "But our job is pretty cool too!"

Truthfully, she'd missed Camp Minerva. Yes, she loved Jessica and Jay, but here she didn't have to hide who she really was. She noticed the others were grinning, too, and realized they probably felt the same way she did.

Maddie and the others ran down the path of crushed seashells lined with pink and red hibiscus flowers, past wooden cabins, sports fields, a climbing wall and ropes course, and a lake with a waterslide.

"Remember when we got attacked by piranhas in that lake?" Maddie asked with a shudder.

"Technically, they were vegetarians," said Caleb.

Lexi made a face. "They didn't *look* like vegetarians at the time."

They all laughed, and Doug sighed wistfully, clearly jealous of their dangerous training exercise.

Familiar buildings emerged from the lush island greenery, based on architecture from every culture and historical time period, including a Japanese-style shrine with gold accents, a Roman-style stone building with marble columns, and even a small English-style castle with turrets and a little drawbridge. Maddie's favorites were the Egyptian and Aztec pyramids—one with smooth edges, the other with zigzag, stepped edges.

Caleb looked down at his S.M.A.R.T.W.A.T.C.H. "We just got a message from Sefu. He's here too and wants to meet us in the Chow Hall," he said.

"The Chow Hall!" Lexi said. "They have the best cucumber soufflé. I hope it's on today's menu! Back home, my brothers and I always arm-wrestle for the last piece."

They approached the squat wooden building, which looked like it was about to disintegrate in the tropical humidity. But Maddie knew from experience that there was much more to this building than met the eye. The screen doors whisked open, revealing a modern glass ceiling supported by wooden beams, in a style that could best be described as summer-camp-meets-tech-company. Sefu stood just inside, with a shy smile on his face.

"Sefu!" Maddie, Lexi, Caleb, and Doug all rushed over and gave him a huge group hug.

"Thanks for guiding us through that last mission!" Maddie said.

"Psh, it was easier than Level Eighteen of BitSmash," Sefu said. "Which is the final level. It's actually quite hard." He looked at his friends. "You must be starving!"

The five of them found an empty picnic table with a centerpiece of colorful orchids. Each place setting had a cloth napkin folded into a complicated shape, and an array of silverware, chopsticks, and other utensils.

A short robot that looked like an exclamation point zoomed up to their table on a central wheel, offering a tray with glasses of lemonade in its little robot arms. It was painted black and white, as if it was wearing a tiny tuxedo. "Beep boop!" the TuxBot said cheerfully as they each grabbed a glass. Doug chugged his.

"Ahh," he said, wiping his mouth with his hand. "My mom forced me to make a lemonade stand to meet kids in my neighborhood, but this stuff tastes way better than what I made."

"At least you learned how to run a small business, right?" asked Caleb.

"No," answered Doug. "In two days, I ended up losing seventy-four dollars. Lemons and stands are expensive!"

Laughing, the friends caught up on their lives since their last letters. Lexi gave detailed updates on her family's cucumber farm, the tiny changes in soil pH levels, the latest crop yield, and a new recipe for cucumber pâté. Sefu had found a list of the one hundred greatest video games of all time and beaten every single one, so he started developing games himself. He had one on the market already and was working on three others. Caleb had started a side gig solving minor mysteries for his classmates at school, like finding lost lunch boxes, and had accidentally solved a decades-long cold case for the local police while searching for a missing retainer.

Out of everyone, Doug was having the hardest time. Before finally being named a member of the Illuminati, he had obsessively researched everything he could about the secretive organization. But now that he had to keep his involvement (and the Illuminati itself) a total secret, he'd struggled to find another interest. He'd tried all sorts of hobbies—scrapbooking, joining the chess club at school, learning how to make his own silly putty . . . but nothing kept his interest.

"Maybe you should take up bird-watching," Lexi suggested.

Doug shuddered. "No way," he said. "I'm scared of pigeons."

"*Forse dovresti studiare l'italiano,*" said Caleb.

"Huh?" said Doug.

Caleb repeated the phrase in English. "Perhaps you could study Italian," he said. "I learned it over the winter. The Illuminati provide tapes so you can learn it in your sleep."

"I don't want to learn in my sleep!" replied Doug. "That's the one time I can relax!"

Maddie shared updates on all her latest inventions—her handheld ice-cream melt-preventer, her automatic French-braid machine (a total disaster, which nearly pulled out a chunk of her hair the first time she used it), and a prototype for X-ray-vision sunglasses that needed more work.

She also showed off the most recent upgrades she'd

made to her hyper-phone. "It still looks just like an ordinary smartphone," Lexi said.

"I know!" said Maddie. "But I recently added a multivalent-ion battery for near limitless power, an ultra-powerful flash for taking night shots, and even an air ionizer to help me sleep better."

"Oh," Lexi mumbled, still staring at the ordinary-looking phone. "But what if you lose it? Or somebody steals it? They'd have all your tech!"

"I can always turn on 'skunk mode,'" said Maddie. "The phone's speaker can give off a smell so terrible, anyone close to it will run away gagging."

All of a sudden, a dark shadow passed over their picnic table, accompanied by a waft of expensive cologne.

"Speaking of skunks—" Maddie scrunched her nose and turned to look.

It was Killian, resplendent in his signature black turtleneck, immaculately pressed trousers, and a gleaming belt buckle in a custom *K* shape that probably cost more than Jessica and Jay's monthly rent. He was taller than the last time Maddie had seen him, and the expression on his face was even more conceited than she remembered.

"You again," he sighed, gesturing to the whole table with a disdainful smirk. "I thought maybe you'd wash out of this program. After all, you're not exactly Illuminati material." Even though his words were rude, his British accent made them sound so polite. "However, I've found no other open seats and am forced to join you." He sat down, snapping his fingers toward the nearest TuxBot.

"Hi, Killian," Maddie said, determined not to let his snooty attitude affect her.

"I'm sure you're all dying to know what I've been up to. In fact, I'm in between assignments. I can't even tell you about them, because none of you worker bees have the high-level security clearance *I* have."

"We're all at the same security clearance," Caleb muttered. Doug nodded emphatically. Sefu tried to slink under the table.

"What was that?" Killian asked with a sneer. He'd been looking away, searching impatiently for a TuxBot to take his dinner order.

"We're all at the same security clearance!" yelled Lexi.

"There's no need to shout. You Americans are so . . . loud." Killian sniffed. "I suppose your undignified tendencies are why they put you in a unit together in the first place."

Maddie felt her face get hot. He was talking about her *friends*. As Killian launched into a cryptic rundown of all the super secret missions he'd been assigned in the last months, Maddie frowned. *Ugh, he's so obnoxious. He needs to be taught a lesson.* Then she typed quickly on her hyper-phone under the dining table. She hacked into the TuxBots' operating system, and with a few keystrokes, made a few minor—okay, major—adjustments to the code that controlled the roving robo-butlers. Pressing her lips together to stop herself from giggling out loud, Maddie slipped her phone back into her pocket without anyone noticing.

". . . and so, that's how I saved a *very* important member of the royal family from a swarm of radioactive hornets," Killian was saying, looking extremely pleased with himself. "I received a secret commendation for my stunning act of bravery. Like a knighthood but better." He looked around the Chow Hall for a TuxBot. "You stupid machines! Someone needs to take my order—*now!*"

A TuxBot rolled up to the table. Just as Killian opened his mouth to order, the TuxBot zoomed away again. "What the—" Killian said. He got up and started speed-walking toward the TuxBot, his pompadour bouncing with every step. But the bot always stayed just a few feet out of his reach and never brought him any lunch. Killian grew redder and redder as his impatience peaked, trying to flag down *any* TuxBot, but they all zoomed away from him. The five super spies looked at each other and burst into laughter, and Maddie accidentally snorted.

"What did you do?" Caleb asked her.

"Oh, nothing," she said, grinning. "Just a little breakthrough in advanced artificial intelligence. I reprogrammed the TuxBots to have free will. So now they'll only serve who they want to."

Killian turned. His face was redder than a fire hydrant.

"You find this amusing, do you?" he snarled. "Let me guess. Pathetic little Maddie, always interfering where she's not wanted. Even Zander Lyon said you were an annoying little gnat."

The laughter at Maddie's table stopped abruptly. Killian's words stung. Although Maddie knew he was a stuck-up, entitled, and overall unpleasant human being, Killian's insult reminded her of how much she'd looked up to Zander Lyon and how much he'd disappointed her. Even worse, the idea of being an annoying gnat brought back the moments she felt lost and alone without her parents, or worried she was a burden on Jessica and Jay. Her cheeks burned as everyone in the Chow Hall stared at her and Killian.

Killian straightened his shoulders and strode toward the exit. He turned and glowered at Maddie. "I *never* forget a slight, Maddie Robinson. You better watch out."

If there was one thing she knew, it was that bullies responded only to strength. So she straightened her own shoulders, looked him straight in the eyes, and said with as much confidence as she could muster, "Do your worst, Killian Horne. Do your worst."

CHAPTER 6

**Maggiore è l'ostacolo, più grande sarà
la gloria nel superarlo.**
The greater the obstacle, the more glory in overcoming it.

Each of the super spies found a reason to stay overnight. Maddie wanted to do research with hard-light holograms found only on the island, Lexi wanted to spar with some black belts who lived there, Sefu wanted access to the island's supercomputer to run a zombie outbreak simulation, and Caleb was convinced there was a treasure hidden inside the island's Egyptian-style pyramid.

Doug didn't bother to come up with an excuse to stay. "We're on a tropical island!" he explained. "Why would I ever want to leave?" Thankfully, the Illuminati had thought of everything. A single push on their

S.M.A.R.T.W.A.T.C.H.es and their families would get texts from "a friend from school's parent" asking if a homework session could become a sleepover. Maddie always felt a little guilty that she wasn't at a friend's house like Jessica thought, but sharing a floating bunk bed with Lexi was pretty close.

The next morning, brilliant sunshine streamed through the mosquito netting of Maddie's cabin. She stretched luxuriously on the top bunk of her bed, which hovered magnetically above the floor. She didn't want to get up. Today, they were all supposed to pack and head to their respective homes, awaiting their next Illuminati mission. But it had felt so good to be reunited with Caleb, Lexi, Sefu, and Doug. To be part of a team again. To not have to hide who she was, and to use her skills to do some real good in the world. She couldn't imagine going back to Philly, where it would be gray and rainy and lonely. She sighed. She would definitely miss Camp Minerva. Especially the Chow Hall, which was *loads* better than her school's cafeteria. *The food here is only wet when it's supposed to be,* she thought.

An urgent knocking at the cabin door broke Maddie out of her thoughts. She opened the door to find Doug, breathless, in Illuminati-issued pajamas with a golden triangle print. His hair was standing up in all directions, and he was wearing only one shoe.

"We're to report to the Obelisk immediately!" he gasped.

"Slow down," Maddie said. "Do you need your inhaler?"

"Come on!" he said. "Everyone's already heading over."

"Okay," Maddie said. "I'll meet you there. But Doug, you'd better get dressed!"

Doug looked down at his pajamas and shoeless foot.

"Oh," he said. "Good idea!"

"Hurry!" Maddie called after him. She roused Lexi and quickly pulled on an Illuminati-issued blue jumpsuit with gold stripes down the arms and legs. She hurried down the path, right behind Lexi, who was still shaping her blue hair into its trademark spikes. They reached the tall glass tower together, where Caleb and Sefu waited. Doug appeared right behind them, this time fully dressed, though his hair was still poking up at wild angles.

"Any idea what this is about?" Maddie asked with a gulp. "I mean, we saved Chase Chance, which is good. . . ."

"But we broke that utility pole . . . ," said Lexi.

"And destroyed a farmer's field," noted Doug.

"I assume Volkov is mad that we didn't stop the tornado even sooner," said Caleb.

Maddie wasn't afraid of Volkov, but she knew that as the woman in charge of every Illuminati agent, Volkov could end their careers as super spies with a wave of her hand. *And she seems like she'd enjoy doing it*, Maddie thought.

"Let's not keep the Grand Sentinel waiting," she said nervously.

The five of them entered the all-glass elevator and

were whisked to the top of the Obelisk, passing totally see-through floors with various Illuminati officials in blue or gold robes typing at computers, consulting thick books and scrolls, or meeting in all-glass conference rooms. It was a jarring mix of ancient and modern technology. Maddie loved it. She wished she could stop off at every floor and find out what everyone was working on.

At the very top, the elevator opened.

A tall woman in a severe blue jumpsuit with pointy shoulders and tall black boots awaited them. She had high cheekbones, her hair was swept up into a tight chignon, and her left eye glinted red. Instead of an eyeball, she had a jeweled optical implant that gave her infrared vision, night vision, and dozens of other upgrades, including, somehow, the ability to see straight behind her.

Next to her stood a nondescript man in a rather forgettable suit. Maddie thought he looked vaguely familiar but couldn't place him.

"Greetings," Volkov said, in a clipped, commanding voice.

"Greetings," Caleb, Sefu, Doug, and Lexi said in unison.

Maddie stifled a nervous giggle. "Hi," she said.

"And may I reintroduce my colleague, Archibald Archibald."

The man, with a stern face and kind eyes—or maybe it was a kind face with stern eyes— straightened his shoulders.

"Please call me Archibald," he said, smiling.

"Wait, is Archibald your first name or your last name?" Doug asked.

"Yes," replied Archibald Archibald.

Doug's confused look stiffened.

Maddie waved, and Archibald Archibald nodded. He was the person who'd recruited her into the Illuminati. Even if she never recognized him, they were sort of friends.

Volkov cleared her throat. "I have summoned you here to give you a special mission."

Maddie felt a smile bloom on her face. A special mission!

Caleb and Maddie caught each other's eyes. She could tell he was feeling the same mix of excitement and nervousness that she was.

Volkov continued, "Normally I'd send in Archibald and his team for something this important, but even though they are masters at disguise, this mission requires youthful agents."

"Cool!" said Doug.

"Why kids?" Caleb asked.

"We need you to blend in with Chase Chance's entourage and fan base. And, since you did such an excellent job with the tornado, Chase has personally requested your services to be his elite bodyguard team for the rest of his worldwide tour. As always, we will craft perfect alibis for your whereabouts."

"OMG, ARE YOU SERIOUS?" Lexi shouted. "This is going to be the Best. Mission. Ever!"

"Not so fast," Volkov said. "This is simply a cover for a super secret mission."

"A super secret mission!" Doug whispered. "Yes!"

"This will be no walk in the park," warned Archibald. "There are powerful forces at work, and they are targeting Chase Chance. This mission is going to take all your cunning, teamwork, and courage." He looked at Maddie. "But as the French playwright Molière reminds us, 'The greater the obstacle, the more glory in overcoming it.'"

Maddie felt a familiar flutter of excitement and nerves in the pit of her stomach. She *knew* her gut feeling was right about all those peculiar things. They weren't just coincidences. Something was happening to Chase Chance. Someone was after him. Someone powerful. And villainous.

"So, what's the objective?" she asked.

"The mission is twofold," said Volkov. "First, you must protect Chase Chance."

"Makes sense," said Caleb. "His fans are . . . I was going to say 'intense,' but I think 'frenzied' is a better word for it."

"Not from overexcited fans!" said Volkov. Caleb's shoulders shrank. "From these very unusual and dangerous threats to his life. We have reason to believe the tornado in Pennsylvania, and the sinkhole, and the deranged birds weren't acts of nature. They were . . . orchestrated. We fear that Chase may be in grave danger from an evil foe. As a star who draws enormous crowds of innocent people, we *must* protect him. And most important of all, you must get to the bottom of what's causing these disasters and who is behind them!"

Maddie exchanged glances with the rest of her team. To get to the bottom of this, they'd have to figure out who would want to hurt Chase . . . and why. If they could find out how these events were engineered, they could zero in on the perpetrator. They'd have to investigate a multitude of angles—geology, topography, meteorology—as well as look into everyone who had access to Chase, his tour bus, and each venue, and thousands of other details to figure out how these not-so-natural disasters kept happening around Chase.

"Do you have any leads? Any idea why Chase is being targeted?" she asked.

"None. You'll have to explore every lead, in every city on the tour," Volkov said sternly. "After everything that happened with Zander Lyon, I think it goes without saying: Don't trust anyone."

Maddie and her team looked at one another. It wasn't

much to go on. In fact, it was *nothing* to go on. The super spies would have to use every single tool and every ounce of training at their disposal.

But if there was one thing that defeating Zander Lyon had taught Maddie, it was that she and her friends could do anything. She looked Volkov in the eye. "We won't let you down."

CHAPTER 7

Chi dorme non piglia pesci.
One who sleeps doesn't catch fish.

The super spies spent another full day on the island, this time researching Chase, the cities on his tour, and even ancient reports of strange and impossible "natural disasters" from the Illuminati's books of secret history.

That night, back in her cabin, Maddie climbed up to the top bunk. Lexi was out late doing evasion training with a group of tactical experts on the island, leaving Maddie alone with her thoughts.

She pulled her neon-green sweater over her pajamas; since the island air was cool, the sweater felt almost as comfy as a hug from her cousin Jessica. She wondered what Jessica and Jay were doing right this moment—probably making dinner and chatting about their days at work. Then Maddie remembered her own parents in their old house, laughing in the kitchen and singing along to obscure French musicals as they cooked. The last time Maddie had seen them, they'd hugged her tightly before heading off to the airport for their expedition to the Arctic Circle. She felt a prickling behind her eyes and smooshed her face into her pillow so no tears would roll out.

At least the pillow was supersoft, and so was the mattress, crafted from high-tech foam invented in outer space by Zander Lyon himself. He'd made a fortune with his futuristic bedding line, which he advertised solely on podcasts, before he turned totally evil. Maddie scowled at the thought of how she had looked up to Zander Lyon and his technology empire. She'd even read his biographies! The thought made her hot with embarrassment. She had been so seriously wrong about him. Everyone had.

A soft *ping* broke the silence. Maddie's hyper-phone lit up with a text from Jessica.

Hey, Maddie! Hope you're having a great time. The principal called and reminded me about the sixth-grade whale-watching trip. I can't believe I totally blanked on that! Jay dropped off a bag with your pj's and toothbrush at school, and the custodian said he'd bring it to you. Is your sweater warm enough? <3<3<3

Of course the Illuminati had already come up with an airtight excuse for why Maddie had never returned home. She started tapping out a reply, then paused, trying to figure out what to write. She didn't want to lie to Jessica, but since she was on a super secret mission, she couldn't spill the beans and tell her *everything*. She stuck with the truth:

I'm great! The sweater is suuuuper warm! And I definitely didn't spill cream cheese all over it! ILU!

Okay, so that's mostly *the truth*, Maddie thought. She put down her phone and stretched out onto the bed, closing her eyes.

Last year, when Maddie was being trained at Camp Minerva and going on her first mission, her cousin thought she was spending the summer at a fancy international camp for gifted students. Would this Illuminati assignment last that long? If she missed a big chunk of the school year, she'd have a *lot* of homework to make up. Would she have to retake all the tests and quizzes? Would she still be able to do her project on Leonardo da Vinci? She'd been pretty interested in that history project and really wanted to know more about the genius inventor who seemed so ahead of his time.

It made her wonder: Was he Illuminati too?

Maddie's curiosity got the better of her. She sat up in bed and pulled up her Illuminati-issued holo-tablet, which was as thin as a piece of paper and nearly indestructible. From the Illuminati digital library, she looked up a biography of Leonardo da Vinci. The *real* biography (not the ones available in bookstores) made clear that her suspicions

were correct: "So da Vinci was an Illuminati member after all," Maddie said to herself. "Cool."

As she read, she got less and less sleepy, and more and more interested—especially when she found out that da Vinci was known for keeping dozens and dozens of notebooks with all his notes, drawings, and inventions. That made her smile. As high-tech and gadget-obsessed as Maddie was, she loved to write down her ideas on actual paper too.

Da Vinci had studied and recorded information on everything from plants to the human body to weather systems to the stars—along with drafting blueprints for futuristic-looking weapons and flying machines. He'd even designed some of the world's first robots! Maddie had no idea that people were even thinking about robots five hundred years ago! Then again, she also knew from discovering Benjamin Franklin's high-tech underground bunker that some figures in history had been much more advanced than they let on.

According to this biography, only eight thousand of da Vinci's notebook pages had survived. *Only?!* Maddie wondered if she would ever have that many ideas. But did that mean other pages hadn't survived—or hadn't been found . . . *yet*? There could be thousands more somewhere!

The book went on to explain rumors that these lost pages contained plans for all kinds of world-changing inventions. There were also rumors that these notebooks were not lost, but *hidden,* so that da Vinci's knowledge would not fall into the wrong hands. What would be revealed in those lost notebooks? And where were they?

Maddie typed *Lost da Vinci Notebooks* into the digital archives search bar and clicked enter, eager to learn more. An all-red screen popped up, with the word *RESTRICTED* in block letters flashing on the screen. Maddie read the smaller text underneath. *SECURITY ALERT! IN-PERSON VIEWING ONLY BY CLEARANCE LEVEL TEN AND ABOVE.*

Maddie squinted at the screen. Her curiosity was piqued. What was so important that it couldn't be stored on the island's top secret, super-unhackable digital cloud, and could only be seen in person at the Illuminati library? Something very secret, or very dangerous.

Or possibly both.

Even though it was just past midnight, Maddie knew she'd never sleep until she found out more. She quickly messaged Sefu, hoping he'd still be awake. She had a feeling he'd be up late gaming.

Meet me at library? Looking for hidden treasure. Will bring snacks.

He pinged her back immediately.

I'm up. Just need to finish this level.

Maddie smiled and hopped down from her bunk. She grabbed a few Illuminati snack bars made out of algae (*Tastes like chocolate!* proclaimed the wrapper) and stuffed them in her pockets. With the pale glimmer of moonlight lighting her way, Maddie jogged past the mostly empty cabins. Camp Minerva was cooler—and quieter—at night. All she could hear were her own footfalls on the crushed-shell path, and the distant chirping of tree frogs in the darkness.

She turned left toward a building fronted with soaring columns, which was modeled after the ancient Egyptian library of Alexandria. She stepped into the cool marble entryway and found Sefu waiting. He was also in his pajamas and sneakers. Maddie noticed his wireless gaming headset peeking through his dark hair.

They nodded to each other and silently headed down an arched hallway to the reference room. There were ornate mahogany desks where Illuminati librarians worked during the day.

"Where should we start?" Maddie whispered, looking around the room. There were flat-screen computer panels, wooden card catalogues with tiny drawers, and shelves full of thick books, binders, and baskets of thumb drives and old-fashioned computer disks.

"How about right here?" Sefu asked, pointing to a hand-painted sign that said *Start Here* with an arrow pointing to one of the antique wooden card catalogues. "You told me we were looking for hidden treasure. Perhaps you could be a bit more specific."

"We're looking for the lost notebooks of Leonardo da Vinci," Maddie said.

Sefu stifled a gasp and smiled. "Let's see—let's try *D* for 'da Vinci,'" he said.

Maddie tugged on the little metal handle of the drawer marked *D*. As the long, skinny drawer rolled out, a metallic hiss reverberated below Maddie's and Sefu's feet. Slowly, the marble floor beneath them began to descend.

"What's happening?" Sefu asked, grabbing on to Maddie for balance.

"I'm not sure!" Maddie replied.

A few seconds later, they found themselves in a glass-walled room, about ten feet below the floor. Beyond the walls was a thick white mist. Out of the mist strode a woman in a long, dark skirt and vaguely Victorian-looking blouse. "Hello, I'm Dewey," she said. "How can I help you?"

"Umm . . . Can *we* help *you?*" Maddie asked, wondering why this woman was trapped behind glass in a misty room underground.

"Oh! No, let me properly introduce myself. I'm the digital interface for the library's unique cataloguing system." She smiled. The effect was friendly, if a little uncanny.

"I am flabbergasted," Sefu said. "You?"

"Double-flabbergasted," Maddie said. She looked at the woman, trying to decipher whether she was a projection or some sort of hologram. "So you aren't a real person?"

"Well, my outward appearance is based on May Seymour, one of the first people to develop the Dewey decimal system, and she was a real person. But I am a digitally created user interface, with terabytes of data, trained and developed by real live librarians to help researchers like you."

"I'd love to get a look at your code," said Maddie.

Dewey simply smiled politely again. "Now then," she said, "what are you looking for?"

"Da Vinci's lost notebooks," Maddie said.

The mist beyond the glass swirled and solidified into a map of Italy. The map grew larger until a tiny town labeled *Vinci* came into view. Images flashed before Maddie and Sefu's eyes: a stern-looking man in a cloak, famous paintings, sculptures, familiar diagrams, lines of funny-looking handwritten text. There was a soft chime, and words formed in the air.

Lost notebooks, da Vinci.

Dewey narrated her findings: "Approximately eight to fifteen thousand pages of notes are currently considered to be lost, destroyed, or hidden."

"'The topics of these pages range from studies of flight, transportation, geometry, and agriculture to warfare, weather, biology, and hydrology. Da Vinci also had a secret codex, with early blueprints for devices associated with space travel, time travel, teleportation, and predicting the future.'"

Maddie and Sefu turned to stare at each other, eyes wide. Clearly da Vinci had more up his sleeve than paint.

"Did she say space travel?" Sefu asked.

Maddie nodded, then asked, "Where is da Vinci's secret codex?"

More words formed in the air. Dewey read them aloud: "'Da Vinci's secret codex. Existence: Confirmed. Current location: Unknown.'"

Maddie stared at the words. So the secret notebook *did* exist. Somehow, over the centuries, the Illuminati had confirmed its existence—maybe even had it at one point. But did that mean that things like time travel and predicting the future were actually possible? And had been invented five hundred years ago? Maddie's mind reeled. If this were true, that meant da Vinci had solved major technological mysteries centuries before anyone else. And if that were true, why didn't the world know about it?

"Are there copies? Photos? Anything?" Maddie asked, desperate to know more.

The words swirled to form new shapes, just as Dewey let out a high-pitched yelp. "RESTRICTED INFORMATION," Dewey shouted.

Maddie looked at Dewey. "But we're clearance Level Ten!"

"RESTRICTED INFORMATION. RESTRICTED INFORMATION. RESTRICTED INFORMATION."

Maddie whipped out her hyper-phone. Maybe she and Sefu could hack into the system, get around this digital firewall, and find out more about that secret notebook! If there were blueprints for these devices, Maddie could build them! Even if the plans weren't perfect, she could improve the designs with modern technology and *make them work!* Her mind whirled with the possibilities. If she could go back in time, she knew the first thing she would do: stop her parents from leaving on that research trip and disappearing.

Just then, Dewey opened her mouth and shrieked, raising a hand to shoo Sefu and Maddie out of the glass-walled room as the walls went blank. "RESTRICTED INFORMATION! LEVEL TWENTY AND ABOVE!" Dewey's kind librarian voice was gone, replaced by something harsh. An alarm sounded.

Maddie slid her phone back into her pocket, and she and Sefu backed slowly away from Dewey as the floor rose back up. They'd gotten very close to finding out something super secret, ultra-classified, and very important. Something very powerful people in the Illuminati wanted to keep hidden—even from their own members.

Maddie knew she should leave well enough alone. The Illuminati usually had a very good reason for keeping their secrets.

Yet somehow, simply knowing that da Vinci's secret notebook existed made Maddie want to learn about it even more.

CHAPTER 8

Non tutte le ciambelle riescono col buco.
Not all doughnuts come out with a hole.

The next morning, Maddie met her crew on the beach, where their minivan sat waiting for them. Seagulls flew overhead in the sunshine, and the waves crashed softly on the shore. Maddie wished they could stay there longer. She wanted to spend more time with Dewey in the Illuminati library. The idea of some forbidden, hidden information about da Vinci's notebooks tantalized her. If she could just get back to the library, she was sure she and Sefu could hack their way past the digital security barriers.

Then they'd be able to find out what earth-shattering inventions da Vinci had designed—and more information on the last known whereabouts of those notebooks.

Even if just one of those inventions worked, it would be amazing. Maddie could think of a million different ways to use a future-predicting device, a time travel machine, and even teleportation to make the world a better place.

But a little voice inside her reminded her of the deeper reason she was so keen to find that intel: What if she could go back in time and see her parents again? What if she could predict the future, to see if she'd ever be reunited with them? She would give anything to be able to do that.

But they had a mission, and the mission always came first. Volkov saluted them by making a triangle with her hands, and gestured to the pile of supplies waiting in the sand. There were backpacks, fannypacks, snackpacks, extra jumpsuits, and an array of new super spy gadgets and secret Illuminati technology that would help them on their mission. Maddie, Caleb, Lexi, and Doug loaded everything into the back of the van. Sefu had decided to set up a mission headquarters at Camp Minerva, so he could use the Illuminati supercomputing systems to run analyses for the team and handle any necessary hacking and communications needs through the Illuminati's top secret ultra-secure satellite link.

Volkov cleared her throat. Everyone knew that meant: *pay attention.* Her jeweled eye glinted in the tropical sun, but her expression was serious. "I cannot overstate the importance of this mission. It is imperative that you get to the bottom of these mysterious 'accidents' before Chase

Chance or his fans get hurt . . . or worse. Use any means necessary to find out who is behind this—and stop them!" She clapped Maddie on the shoulder and looked deep into her eyes. Maddie stood up straighter. She certainly did *not* want to let Volkov down. The team saluted Volkov and hopped into the minivan.

Lexi read from their mission brief, a slip of paper that Volkov had handed to her before the doors closed.

"'Mission Step One: Meet Chase Chance at his first tour stop in Paris. This message will self-destru—'" Lexi read as the paper disintegrated in her hands.

"Next stop, Paris!" whooped Doug. The minivan swooped up into the sky.

As they flew, Maddie told the others about her and Sefu's midnight library visit, what they'd discovered—and what they had been prevented from discovering. She got more and more excited as she explained that da Vinci might have created blueprints to world-changing inventions.

"But what does that have to do with our mission?" asked Lexi, who always focused on the practical. Maddie paused, a bit deflated. She'd hoped her friends would be just as curious as she was. But she knew her own private reasons were just that—her own private reasons.

"Don't you think it's odd that we're not supposed to know about it? Don't you want to know?" she asked, appealing to their sense of adventure.

"You know I love a good mystery," said Caleb. "But if

you haven't noticed, we're on a very important mission to protect a very important person. That should be our priority for now."

"I guess you're right," Maddie said slowly, as she made a connection in her mind. "But what if—what if—we could find da Vinci's blueprints, then build his inventions? We could certainly use any of those secret inventions to help us protect Chase!"

"Interesting hypothesis," said Caleb. "I suppose, if we had a future-prediction device, we could look for irregularities, narrow down the parameters. . . ."

"We could know ahead of time when and where these freak occurrences would happen," Lexi said.

"And keep Chase away from them!" said Doug.

"We could stake out the area where the accidents are supposed to happen, see who shows up, record any suspicious activity, and find out what's causing them," Lexi said.

"Exactly! We could stop whoever is doing this!" Maddie said. "And think of all the bad things we can prevent from happening!"

"That's a great idea in *theory*," Caleb said. "But our *actual* mission is to accompany Chase on tour and protect him. We can't just go off to find this stuff."

"And what if the blueprints you're looking for don't actually exist? It could be a wild-goose chase," said Lexi. "And not the fun kind of wild-goose chase, like when we have to chase down a wild goose on the farm."

Maddie thought for a moment. "Well, while we're on tour, we're going to be in some of the same places where da Vinci lived and worked. So maybe we can look for his blueprints *while* we protect Chase. Sort of a side mission."

"A side mission?" Doug said, grinning. "That's so Illuminati." The minivan started descending, and they passed through a layer of fluffy white clouds. "I'm in . . . as long we're still keeping Chase safe. He's so cool!" The rest of the team nodded in agreement.

"I'll check Chase's digital footprint and do a data analysis of past incidents to see what patterns I can find," Sefu said, through the speakers.

"I'll study the local conditions—the weather, the water, measure radiation levels. Maybe something weird geologically or meteorologically is happening," Lexi said.

"I'll use my not-inconsiderable powers of observation to uncover anomalous behavior by anyone close to Chase," Caleb said.

"Powers of observation?" asked Doug. "You mean, like, looking around?"

Caleb shrugged. "That's certainly a less exciting way of putting it," he said. "Besides, ninety percent of sleuthing is just looking around!"

"I'll try to come up with some inventions that can protect Chase—and all his fans—if and when the next weird thing happens," said Maddie.

"What should I do?" said Doug. "It seems like you guys

have everything covered." He sounded rather put-out.

"You're the best researcher I've ever met," Maddie said. "Trust me, we need you. And since we don't know what's going to happen, we need everyone to be on high alert for anything suspicious."

"Okay, that I can handle," Doug said. "Plus, maybe Chase will need an extra backup dancer!" He busted a move in his seat while his fellow agents did their best to look elsewhere.

Soon the top of the Eiffel Tower appeared on the horizon, soaring above the city of Paris.

"We're almost there!" Doug said, practically bursting with enthusiasm.

As the minivan swooped lower, Maddie heard the hiss of the invisibility shields lowering. She gazed at the gray rooftops and cathedral spires and the tree-lined boulevards.

"It's true what they say about Paris. It's beautiful," she said.

Caleb nodded. "I've been here with my parents and it never gets old. I—" He stopped himself, remembering that Maddie didn't have parents to travel with. "Sorry, Maddie. I didn't mean to . . ."

"It's all right," Maddie said. "Paris is actually where my parents had their honeymoon. They used to show me their old photos—eating croissants and drinking tiny cups of coffee, smiling in front of Notre-Dame cathedral. They promised to bring me here one day." Maddie missed her parents intensely, but she didn't want to make her friends upset. "But I'm glad I get to be here with all of you!"

"Likewise," Caleb said.

"Definitely," Lexi added.

"I'm just happy to be anywhere with anyone," Doug said.

The sun was high in the sky when the minivan landed on the roof of Le Zénith, a concert hall on the outskirts of Paris. Maddie pushed her thoughts of her parents to the back of her mind as the team split up to secure the location before Chase's arrival that evening.

Inside the venue, Maddie opened her hyper-phone and activated a scanning app that would identify any human being who might be hidden and up to no good. She spent an hour going over every inch of the stage and the massive seating area before heading backstage to Chase's dressing room.

She didn't need her phone to notice something was different. "Looks like the color consultant had an epiphany," Maddie said to herself. The entire room, even the trampoline, was covered in red velvet. Maddie snuck a handful of red M&M's out of Chase's bowl and stuffed them into her mouth. "Anybody see anything strange yet?" she said into her earpiece, her mouth half-full.

"Nothing here," said Lexi. "I'm testing all of Chase's props. The revolving dance floor. The giant disco ball he steps out of when he comes onstage. It's all normal so far. Well, as normal as a giant disco ball can be."

"What about the pyrotechnics?" asked Maddie.

"I confirmed with security that no one has touched the air cannons, the fire cannons, or the glitter cannons except Chase's regular team," said Lexi.

"And Doug and I just interviewed every roadie, dance crew member, backup singer, and musician," Caleb said. "If they work for Chase, we talked to them. Did you know that Chase's massage therapist has his own manicurist?"

"Gotta have clean fingers if you're gonna touch Chase," added Doug. "Besides, they all seem to love Double-C! That's my nickname for Chase."

"Their body language and eye movements indicated to me that they were telling the truth. All of his employees really like Chase," said Caleb.

The super spies reconvened backstage. "Sefu, have you found anything on your end?" Maddie asked.

"Nothing suspicious," Sefu said into their earpieces. "I've run a social media scan of concertgoers, but no red flags have popped up."

"So . . . that's all good news, then, right?" Maddie said. Her team nodded. "Chase should be safe for tonight's show. Let's go tell him!"

They walked to Chase's dressing room. Maddie knocked softly.

"Be out in one sec," Chase said.

One sec turned into one minute. And then five. And then ten.

At minute twenty-seven, Maddie slid down the wall of the backstage corridor until she sat with her legs splayed out in front of her, leaned her head back, and yawned. She was tired from the flight and preconcert check, and she could tell the others were, too. An hour passed, but Chase still hadn't come out.

Finally, the super spies approached the dressing room door and knocked again. No one answered. "Chase? You almost ready?" Lexi said.

"Go away! I'M MEDITATING!" a voice yelled.

Caleb looked at his watch. "Well, it's five minutes to curtain, and—"

"I SAID, I'M MEDITATING!" Chase's voice sounded like he had *not* been meditating.

"Ohhhh-kay," whispered Maddie. The super spies looked away from Chase's door, taken aback by the superstar's behavior, and waited in silence for several more minutes.

Suddenly, a loud yell came from the other side of the wall. Then a loud *CRASH* as if something hard had shattered.

"What was that?" Doug shouted. The super spies looked at each other in horror. *Chase is in danger!* Lexi broke open the door with a strong heave of her shoulder. Inside, the dressing room was strewn with costumes and fast-food wrappers. A ceramic bowl lay broken on the floor, with red M&M's scattered all over the carpet.

Chase sat casually on a chair, playing on his phone.

"Are you all right?" Maddie asked, worried.

"What happened?" said Doug. "We heard a crash!" Chase looked lazily up from his phone. "Oh, I found a blue M&M mixed in with my red ones," he said.

"So that's why you yelled?" Caleb asked.

"And smashed the bowl?" Lexi asked.

"Well, duh. I'm only supposed to eat *red* food this week. Everyone knows that!" Chase said huffily. "Listen, I operate at a hundred and ten percent at all times. So I can't have my mental and physical equilibriums out of sync for any reason."

Maddie rolled her eyes. Chase was turning out to be quite bratty. And didn't he know that all M&M's tasted the same, no matter what color they were? Maddie made eye contact with Lexi and Caleb, wondering just what they had gotten into, acting as overqualified bodyguards for a spoiled pop star.

Lexi looked confused. "I can't believe you got so mad

about a thing like that! If we wasted food like that on the farm—"

"Whatever," Chase interrupted Lexi, and shooed her away with a dismissive wave. He kicked the side of his red velvet beanbag chair. "Vibe killer," he muttered.

Maddie noticed Lexi's hurt expression. Dealing with Chase's moods on tour was starting to feel like a glorified babysitting job, instead of an important mission. Maddie vowed not to let Chase's attitude get in the way of them getting to the bottom of who was targeting him—and why.

CHAPTER 9

La Gioconda ha la chiave del futuro.
The Mona Lisa holds the key to the future.

After Chase finally got over the Terrible Incident of the Blue M&M and performed for his fans, he met the super spies on the roof of Le Zenith. The young agents were tired from patrolling the venue and nearby streets late into the night. Thankfully, Chase let them ride in his ultra-luxury helicopter to a nearby hotel. The helicopter seats reclined into beds, and there were flat-screen TVs and bowls of strawberries, slices of red velvet cake (minus the white frosting), and, of course, red M&M's scattered about the cabin. Chase collapsed into a seat without a word, pulled a red silk eyeshade over his face, and started snoring. The kids took their seats.

"This is so fancy!" Lexi whispered to Maddie.

"I know!" Maddie said, snuggling down into her reclining seat. She had to admit, even if dealing with Chase was a bit of a headache, the perks of traveling even fancier than first class were pretty sweet. After all, she'd never really been anywhere before becoming an Illuminati agent, and now she was traveling in style.

After a short fifteen-minute trip, they landed at the hotel and checked into a connecting suite of rooms. Maddie pulled up the publicly known digital copies of da Vinci's notebooks on her holo-tab. Lexi, Doug, and Caleb met in Maddie's suite and tried to come up with a plan for the rest of the tour.

"Basically, our job is to stop something from happening to Chase," said Lexi, "but we have no idea what, when, or even why."

Doug scratched his head. "I don't get how we can do that, other than staying by Chase's side twenty-four seven."

"What fun that's turning out to be," said Caleb sarcastically.

"I know! It *is* fun!" said Doug, not picking up on Caleb's sarcasm.

Maddie looked up from her holo-tab, where she had been scouring the internet for any whispers about da Vinci's hidden blueprints. "A way to predict the future sure would come in handy," she said in a singsong voice.

"That would definitely help," admitted Caleb. "But until

we have something like that, we have to figure out what connects these events—no matter how small. Maybe that way we can find a common thread." The super spies sat quietly, thinking.

Maddie knew she should be thinking of how best to protect Chase, but her mind was fixated on da Vinci's secret codex. *If we find that, I could build da Vinci's Future Predictor! And using that, I'll learn if I'll ever see my parents again.* She noticed her friends still focused on the mission at hand. *And keep Chase safe, too, of course,* Maddie reminded herself.

But once she put her mind to something, it was hard for her to think of anything else. And by this point, she was certain that ultimately, the best way to keep the bratty pop star safe—and the whole world, too—was to locate da Vinci's secret notebook.

Wouldn't da Vinci have left some clue about where he hid his most exciting, most futuristic work? Didn't he want his totally awesome, super-futuristic blueprints to be found eventually? wondered Maddie. "Maybe I missed something in the da Vinci notebooks we do have."

Maddie noticed Caleb and Lexi sharing a quick look of disapproval, but they could both sense how determined Maddie was.

She started flipping through the pages of da Vinci's *not*-secret notebooks on her holo-tab as she thought. She was desperate to find some reference or hint to any of da Vinci's *secret* notebook. . . . After going through hundreds of pages in the order da Vinci wrote them, Maddie noticed that sometimes, stray letters would appear, not linked to any of the other words on the page. Maddie felt a touch of excitement—the same feeling she got when faced with an exciting new challenge to figure out.

"You guys? There's something weird here. . . ."

"You mean that you keep checking centuries-old diaries for ways to keep a twenty-first-century superstar safe?" asked Caleb.

"No," said Maddie. "Something actually weird."

"What ya got?" asked Lexi, craning her neck over Maddie's shoulder.

"Look here," said Maddie, pointing to a stray *M* found in the bottom corner of a page. "And this isn't the only random letter, either. There are other letters on other random pages."

"So you're saying you think the letters are a clue, then," guessed Caleb.

"Exactly!" said Maddie.

The team crowded around Maddie's holo-tab. She flipped through the pages.

"I'll write them down," Lexi offered. She grabbed a pencil from behind Maddie's right ear and made a list of all the extra letters da Vinci had written:

ꟼƧYUYƆ ƎWꓭ⅃Ǝ ƎWꓭIꓷ ꓭI ꓭƎꓷꟼꓷYH ꓭM

Maddie, Caleb, Lexi, and Doug puzzled over it.

"The letters do seem kind of random," said Lexi.

"Not to mention backward," said Doug.

"Da Vinci wrote backward nearly all the time," explained Maddie.

"Huh?" said Doug and Lexi at the same time.

"Maybe he didn't want anyone to know what he was writing," offered Doug.

"Very possible," said Maddie.

"Let me guess," said Caleb. "Was da Vinci left-handed?"

"He was!" said Maddie. "Wait, how did you know that?"

"Simple deduction," said Caleb. "His notes and illustrations are so precise, I'm sure he couldn't bear to have them smudged, which is a common problem for left-handed writers—unless you were to write backward."

"The backward letters are still gibberish," said Doug.

"Unless they're a code!" said Maddie excitedly.

"Could be a complicated puzzle," said Caleb.

"I don't think so," said Maddie. "I think da Vinci wanted someone to solve this."

The four spies worked together to decipher the message. "I think I cracked it," Caleb said after a few minutes. "Each letter represents the letter just before it in the alphabet. So the first *M* is actually an *L*."

Maddie grabbed her other pencil from behind her left ear and spelled out the message:

LA GIOCONDA HA LA CHIAVE DEL FUTURO

"What's that?" Lexi asked.

"*La Gioconda* is the Italian name for a painting by

Leonardo da Vinci. It's more commonly known as the *Mona Lisa*," said Caleb.

"Whoa," said Doug, raising his eyebrows. "That's, like, the one painting I've heard of. It's SUPER famous!"

"What's the rest of it mean?" asked Lexi.

"That's in Italian, da Vinci's mother tongue," said Caleb. "Thank you, Illuminati language tapes!"

Doug nodded approvingly.

"Don't keep us waiting!" said Lexi. "What's it mean?"

Caleb cleared his throat theatrically, but Maddie had already pulled up her custom translation app on her hyper-phone. The super spies peered at the screen. It said:

THE GIOCONDA HOLDS THE KEY TO THE FUTURE

Maddie felt an electric surge in her veins. Had they just found a clue hidden across da Vinci's notebooks? Maybe this clue would lead them to da Vinci's secrets.

"The key to the future! Do you think this could be a reference to the future prediction device? It must be!" Maddie said, pointing to the word "future."

"It's not impossible," said Caleb.

"Maybe this clue leads to that notebook," Lexi said. "The one with blueprints for the future predicting machine."

"A future-predicting device would be so cool!" said Doug. "We could use it to find out who will win the next World Series! Or when humans will live on Mars! Or what I'll have for lunch!"

Or if I'll ever see my parents again, Maddie thought.

"But first, we'd use it as a tool to complete our mission," Lexi said, keeping the team on track. "Right, everyone?"

"Right," said Maddie.

"We're all agreed, the mission to protect Chase comes first," said Caleb.

"No matter how annoying he is," added Maddie. Lexi and Caleb laughed, but Doug frowned.

"He's under a lot of pressure!" shouted Doug. "If he acts a little bit angry sometimes, it's only because he works so hard to make people happy!"

Maddie put her hand on his shoulder. "Don't worry, Doug," she said. "We won't let anything happen to him. And we'll track down da Vinci's secret notebook, too."

The next night, the team returned to Le Zenith for Chase's second sold-out show. They did another in-depth sweep of the entire venue.

Maddie checked backstage, walking past dancers stretching, backup singers doing vocal exercises, and musicians warming up. She made eye contact with a burly bouncer guarding Chase's dressing room but walked away quickly after he growled at her. "Nothing to report backstage," she said into her earpiece.

Lexi was on the side of the stage as roadies finished last-minute checks of Chase's gear and stage set. "All clear onstage," she reported.

Caleb was roaming the audience as fans began to stream in. "There are an awful lot of people crying out here," he said. "But I think they're just excited for the show to start. Nothing dangerous as far as I can see."

"I just checked all the refreshment stands," said Doug. Over the earpiece, Maddie could hear the slurp, slurp, slurp of soda through a straw. "And I can report that none of the drinks have been poisoned," he said with a burp.

"Sefu?" asked Maddie. "You notice anything?"

"Indeed not," said Sefu, calling in from Camp Minerva. "I've found nothing suspicious in my digital forensics of the ticket holders for this evening, either."

Crowds of kids and teenagers and parents filled the hall, buzzing with excitement. The lights dimmed, and a fog of theatrical mist enveloped the stage. The buzzing of the crowd turned to loud cheering. "Chase! Chase! Chase!" echoed through the cavernous amphitheater. In a flash of magenta and green laser lights, Chase appeared onstage.

"Hey there, Chasers. It looks like you've finally caught me," he crooned into his microphone. The cheering swelled to a deafening roar. Maddie covered her ears and smiled. This was really happening—and it was far cooler than an average day in middle school. She was at a Chase Chance show in Paris, with a prime backstage spot and no tornadoes in sight.

The first notes to Chase's single "I Heart You" poured out from huge speakers, and Chase stood in the spotlight,

gazing soulfully out at the audience. As he sang the first few lines, the crowd screamed and sang along, including Lexi, who seemed to know all the words. As Chase performed each song, Maddie could tell that he was enjoying it as much as the audience, and all traces of his inner brat had disappeared. He seemed to come alive in the stage lights, stared at by thousands of fans who were singing his own lyrics back to him. She even spotted Caleb in the crowd, bobbing his head to some of Chase's catchier beats.

As each song followed the next, it was clear that the concert was proceeding without any weird weather occurrences, bird attacks, or any other detectable danger. Maddie let her shoulders relax. The super spies would likely not have to be heroes tonight.

After several rounds of "all clear" and "nothing suspicious," Maddie began to grow impatient. She wanted to find *La Gioconda* and look for "the key to the future" that da Vinci had hinted at in his notebooks. In her late-night research, she'd discovered that the *Mona Lisa* was right here in Paris, at the Louvre museum, only a few miles away. This might be their only chance to see *La Gioconda* before being whisked off to the next tour stop.

After three encores, Chase was exhausted from his performance. He slouched into his makeup chair and wiped sweat from his face with a fluffy towel. Then he chugged a bottle of iced pomegranate juice. "That show was epic, am I right?" He lifted his hand for a high five. Doug, who was the closest, grinned and gave it a smack.

"Chase," Maddie started, hoping that the star would be in a postshow good mood and not one of his M&M-bowl-smashing moods. "We've had an idea."

"We've had only a few leads on the mysterious events plaguing you—" Caleb said.

"Zero leads," corrected Maddie.

"Okay, *zero* leads on the mysterious events plaguing you," Caleb explained. "So we have to be more proactive."

"Hey, fam, so far, so good. Nothing weird has happened since you joined the tour," Chase said, fixing his hair swoop in the mirror. Then he turned and looked at the super spies. "And it's not like you guys can see the future or anything." He chuckled.

Maddie laughed, a bit nervously. "Ummm . . . funnily enough, we have reason to believe that blueprints to a future-prediction device exist, and that a clue to their location may be hidden right here in Paris," she said. Chase put down his sweaty face towel and looked at her with interest. "We could use it to keep you safe—but we have to find it first," she continued.

Chase's eyes widened. "A future-prediction device? That sounds so cool! I could use it to find out how many Grammys I'll win this year. Or what I'll have for lunch tomorrow!"

"Exactly!" said Doug.

"You need to go find it!" Chase said authoritatively.

"But we can't shirk our duty to protect you, and since you're Illuminati too . . . we'd like you to come with us so that we can keep an eye on you," Lexi said.

Chase frowned. "Sorry, guys. I left it all out on the stage. I gotta do my crystal treatments." He yawned and slumped deeper into his chair.

"But—" Maddie said, trying to think of a way to convince

Chase. They *had* to find that clue before they left Paris!

"I'll stay with him," Doug piped up. "I'll keep an eye on things while you guys check out the lead."

Caleb, Lexi, and Maddie all looked at each other.

"Are you sure this is a good idea?" Lexi asked. "That's a lot of responsibility to put on you, Doug."

"I'm not a baby," Doug said, puffing out his chest. "I can handle this!"

"If anything happens, we can rush right back, okay?" Maddie said. "This structure is secure, the security detail seems to have everything under control, and we might not have a chance like this again."

"Just go, you guys!" Doug said.

"As they say in Paris, *à bientôt!*" said Caleb as the team headed out a side entrance. The main street was crowded with five-star restaurants and glittering nightclubs. Would-be clubgoers snapped selfies as they waited in long lines behind velvet ropes.

Maddie dialed in Sefu and told him the plan.

"I've got the coordinates for the Louvre," Sefu said. "It's only a few miles away."

"But how will we get there?" said Lexi. "I'm happy to run—I haven't gotten a decent workout in since we got here!"

"Well, a cab would be fastest," said Caleb, "but I don't have any euros on me—do you?"

As Maddie shook her head, she noticed a pack of motor

scooters lined up in a row by the curb.

"Maddie," said Caleb, "any chance you could hack the locks so we could borrow those scooters for a bit?"

"Waaaay ahead of you," she said, grinning, her fingers already firing in her hyper-phone's hacking app. "Locks . . . unlocked."

The super spies raced across the street, threw on the helmets strapped to the handlebars, and hopped onto the scooters, then rode off into the night.

Maddie felt like she was driving through a fairy tale. They passed buildings that were hundreds of years old, protected by gold-tipped fences, and public parks that were alive with music and conversation, lit by historic streetlamps. They saw college students arguing passionately in cafés and watched sidewalk postcard dealers pack up their wares for the evening.

Maddie spotted her reflection in the window of a high-end boutique selling handbags and chic sweaters. Some of the sweaters were even funky and neon, like the one Jessica had made her.

What do you know? I'm stylish! Maddie thought.

Riding the electric scooters was easy—after all, Maddie and her team had completed mandatory motorcycle-riding lessons during their training at Camp Minerva.

"Keep going straight for a while," Sefu called into their earpieces.

Maddie felt exhilarated riding with her friends through

Paris at night. She even tried to pop a wheelie on a particularly empty stretch. Lexi tried the same trick—naturally, she balanced perfectly on her back wheel and zoomed in front of Maddie and Caleb.

"Woo-hoo!" Maddie and Caleb cheered. Sometimes being a super spy was awesome.

"Turn right here!" called Sefu, and they all veered off the path onto the right-hand side of a busier street. Soon they were in a neighborhood of elegant cream-colored buildings with ornamented balconies. "You're almost there," said Sefu.

They coasted up to a huge limestone building, circling a clear glass pyramid sticking out of the ground. They hopped off their scooters and gazed up at the most famous museum in the world.

They had arrived at the Louvre.

CHAPTER 10

Non è tutto oro quello che luccica
All that glitters is not gold.

A sign on the revolving glass door said: *Fermé.* Closed.

Which, of course, Maddie had planned for. But what she hadn't planned for were the half-dozen guards patrolling just inside the front door.

"What was your plan for getting in, exactly?" asked Caleb.

"I was going to hack in and disable the electronic security systems, but I didn't count on there being so many guards. We need another way in."

"Can't we come back when it's open?" asked Lexi.

Maddie shook her head. "Chase's tour leaves Paris first thing tomorrow."

Caleb nodded. "So we've got to get in and get out tonight without anyone knowing we were here."

"The museum is home to some of the best security in the world," Sefu said in their earpieces. "For good reason—it houses numerous priceless artworks and historical artifacts."

Maddie's heart sank. They should've used their scooter ride to make a plan instead of taking in the Parisian sights like tourists. Then again, it wasn't her fault Paris was so beautiful!

"Well, if anyone can get in, and get out, it would be some super spies, right?" Maddie said, trying to boost everyone's confidence. "There must be a way in! Volkov always says: when a door is closed, find a window."

"Hmmmm . . . Windows . . . that gives me an idea!" Caleb said. "I think there may be an elegant solution to this puzzle."

He pulled up a hologram of the Louvre's blueprints with his S.M.A.R.T.W.A.T.C.H. as he explained his plan in the public courtyard in front of the Louvre. "There are glass skylights along the top of the museum. If we can get in from above, into one of the less popular exhibit halls, I bet we can avoid the guards." Maddie and Lexi nodded. "Lexi, can you find us an entry point?"

"On it," she said, jogging off.

"Maddie, can you get us on the roof?"

Maddie smiled. "I think I have something for that."

While Lexi scaled a nearby tree for a better vantage

point, Maddie searched in her fanny pack and found a ball of top secret polymer that she'd developed in her lab at home. She fashioned the acid-yellow material into smaller pieces, enough for all of them. It had been inspired by gecko toes—she called it GeckoGrip. They all reconvened, stuck some GeckoGrip to the bottom of their shoes, and conferred for a few minutes, agreeing on the final plan.

Maddie just hoped there were no security guards patrolling this area, or couples canoodling nearby. They had to do this quickly.

She unwrapped a fishing-line skein of diamond nano-cord (a hyper-tensile type of filament inspired by spiderwebs and silkworms). Then she grabbed one of the lime-green metallic lounge chairs that dotted the outskirts of the Louvre and tied the nano-cord around it. She affixed some of her GeckoGrip to the chair's feet. "Think of it like a grappling hook," she said.

She handed the chair to Lexi, who swung it around and around with her right arm, like a pitcher getting ready for a no-hitter. With a soft grunt, she let the chair fly up, up, up, until it landed on the roof. Thanks to Maddie's sticky mixture, the chair's feet bonded immediately to the roof and stayed put even as Lexi tugged on the nano-cord.

"I'll go first," said Maddie, hoping that if she pretended to be confident, then real confidence would follow. They'd done missions before, but for some reason, trying to break

into such an important place made her heart beat a little faster.

Maddie pulled herself up the nano-cord, letting her GeckoGrip toe pads connect with the wall. She pushed herself up step by step, walking up the wall. She knew the GeckoGrip was secure—but didn't dare look down over twenty feet below.

"Are you sure this cord . . . and that chair . . . are strong enough to support us?" asked Caleb, breathing heavily as he climbed behind Maddie.

"Yup!" said Maddie. "That is, if my calculations are correct."

"Well, um, are they?" Caleb said worriedly. "I didn't see you using a calculator down there."

"I think so," said Maddie. "But the truth is, ninety-nine percent of the time you try to invent something, it ends in failure."

"Failure?" asked Caleb, with a gulp.

"Like the one time I totally misjudged the suction power of the solar-powered robot vacuum I made for my cousin,

Jessica. I ended up sucking up half the living room—including the cat. The cat was fine, of course. She still gives me dirty looks, though."

"Was that supposed to be inspirational?" asked Caleb. "Because now I'm just terrified."

Maddie giggled and kept climbing, finally reaching the roof of the famous museum, with Lexi and Caleb right behind her. *Maybe this will be easier than I thought*, she said to herself.

From Illuminati HQ, Sefu attempted to access the museum's internal security systems, while Maddie and her team approached the bank of huge, curved skylights inlaid in the roof. Lexi tugged at the metal frame outlining a corner pane of glass.

"I bet I could break through this glass with one punch!" she whispered.

"I know, but we can't have shattered glass alerting the guards—or left as evidence of our late-night visit," Maddie said.

Lexi grunted, trying to open the pane of windows. When it wouldn't budge, she took out her Illuminati-issued pocket-knife. Using the ultrasharp blade, she cut a circle in the glass, wide enough for one agent at a time to slip through.

Maddie took a deep breath. "Ready?" she asked, to herself as much as to her team.

"Ready," Lexi and Caleb answered, without hesitation.

The kids peered through the hole in the window. The floor seemed very, very far away.

"How many stories high are we?" said Maddie, feeling a flutter of nerves.

"I could tell you," said Sefu in her earpiece, "but I don't think that would be helpful."

"Right, okay. On the count of three," whispered Maddie. "One . . . two . . . Whoa—"

Lexi gathered her nano-cord and dropped it though the hole. Without hesitating, she leaped through the hole and hung from the line of nano-rope, three feet below the others. "C'mon! It's not so scary once you get started."

The others took turns stepping through the opening, holding on tight to the invisibly thin rope. They descended slowly, like three very cautious spiders. The cavernous space was dark, lit only by a few security lights, but Maddie could see some paintings and statues on the marble walls, mostly hidden in shadows. They stayed silent so as not to alert any roving security guards.

When Maddie's feet hit the marble floor, she felt a wave of relief. They each took off their GeckoGrip toe pads. The hanging lines of nano-cord were almost imperceptible in the dark, empty room. Unless someone happened to look up and see the hole in the window, a patrolling guard wouldn't notice anything out of the ordinary.

"Which way?" Lexi asked.

"You're in the Egyptian collection. You need to get to the Denon Wing," Sefu said. "Head downstairs, then west."

The three jogged lightly down the wide hallway, trying

to keep their footfalls as quiet as possible. They turned a corner and ran past several large works of art in ornate frames. Caleb stopped to stare at one.

"Hurry!" Maddie hissed. "We don't have much time."

"But it's a Botticelli!" Caleb said quietly, gesturing at a painting with three female figures presenting a gift to a fourth.

"Psst," Lexi whispered, making a universal *hurry up* gesture.

They ran down the stairs and entered a vast room with wood paneling. In the center, a painting was embedded in a freestanding wall behind a thick pane of plexiglass, with a waist-high curved railing that kept crowds of museumgoers at a safe distance. They approached the railing, taking in the thick gilt frame and the dark painting within. A woman's face and torso emerged from the murky background. She had long, dark hair swept back from her forehead, and a thoughtful, peaceful gaze. A subtle smile graced her face. Maddie, Lexi, and Caleb stared in awe for a moment.

"'*La Gioconda*, aka *La Joconde*, aka the *Mona Lisa*,'" Caleb read from a sign on the wall. "'Painted in the early 1500s by Leonardo da Vinci. Probably an Italian noblewoman, Lisa Gherardini.'"

"Wow," said Lexi. "It's smaller than I pictured it. And what happened to her eyebrows?"

"I wonder what she's thinking about," said Maddie. She

tilted her head from side to side. "It's like she's following us with her eyes."

The three continued to stare at the painting in awe for a few more moments before Caleb interrupted them. "Let's focus," he said. "We need to gather as much data as we can." He stepped forward, pulling a small magnifying glass out of his pocket.

"Wait! Don't get too close." Maddie clicked the infrared setting on her hyper-phone and waved it in front of the *Mona Lisa*. Tiny red laser lines appeared in the field of light emanating from her device. "Lasers, motion sensors, probably tons of other security measures as well. We don't want to trigger an alarm."

The three super spies paced in front of the painting, scrutinizing it. The hidden message in da Vinci's notebooks had told them that the *Mona Lisa* held the key to the future. Maddie shined her flashlight on the masterpiece, hoping that would make it easier to see. But the glare just bounced off the protective plexiglass shield that went from the floor to the ceiling, making it harder to see the painting underneath.

"Does anyone see anything that looks like a key to the future?" Caleb said, peering at the highly protected painting. Maddie dug through her fanny pack, hoping to find a gadget or combination of tools that would help her find some type of clue in the painting. She stared at the blurry greenish-blue landscape in the background of the painting. Was there some sort of pattern hidden in the landscape? It looked like trees or castles over water. Maddie wished she could get closer, but she didn't dare trigger an alarm. But there had to be a way—the *Mona Lisa* was right there! She thought for a moment.

Suddenly, she gasped.

"What?" Lexi whispered.

"I think we can *look* closer, even if we can't *get* closer."

"Huh?" Lexi said.

Maddie grabbed her phone again, fiddled with some toggles and lenses, swiftly switched to a high-tech tele-photo lens, and zoomed in on the painting.

"You guys, check this out!" Maddie panned the lens slowly from side to side. A high-resolution image of *La Gioconda* appeared on her screen. She scanned down the *Mona Lisa*'s hair and forehead, which appeared to be covered by a gossamer-thin veil. Maddie scanned down farther to the face, where she could even see the minuscule cracks in the varnish on the painting.

"She definitely looks like she knows a secret," Lexi said, taking in the thoughtful, mysterious expression. Maddie studied the folds in the *Mona Lisa*'s clothing, so realistic in the interplay of shadow and light. She looked carefully at the folded hands, the wooden arm of a chair, just visible above the bottom edge of the painting. But try as she might, she couldn't find any hidden details in the painting.

"Maybe there's something on the back? Or under the frame?" Lexi said.

"We can't get to it," said Caleb, "without disabling the laser field, hacking into the alarm system, scrambling the video surveillance . . . and we'd still need to get through that glass . . ."

"I could do it," Lexi said, cracking her knuckles.

". . . *without* damaging the painting," Caleb finished.

"Well, it would help if we knew exactly what we were looking for," said Lexi.

"We haven't been able to narrow the parameters of our search very much," admitted Maddie. "It could be a code, a hidden image, a note—we don't know. The message just said '*La Gioconda* holds the key to the future.'"

Caleb examined the intense levels of protection around the painting. "It's too heavily secured. We can't get close enough to find the key," he said, a hint of resignation in his voice.

Maddie wanted to scream. They'd broken into the Louvre. They'd deciphered and followed da Vinci's clue and he'd led them right here.

Only . . . it was a dead end.

CHAPTER 11

Quando il gatto non c'è, i topi ballano.
When the cat isn't there, the mice dance.

"Well, let's take as many photos of the painting itself and this room as we can. I don't think we'll have a chance to come back," Maddie said. She started snapping photos from every angle. As she leaned over the barrier to get a better shot, a jarring buzzing sound blared out from the wall.

"Maddie!" Lexi hissed. "You triggered one of the motion sensors!"

Caleb put his finger to his lips. Everyone froze. The pounding of footsteps echoed off the marble floors. *Someone was coming.* Several someones.

With a heavy clanking sound, the section of wall holding

the *Mona Lisa* sank backward, and two side panels mechanically slid shut, hiding the painting from view.

Maddie pointed to the doorway on the other side of the room. *Let's go*, she mouthed.

The three sprinted as silently as they could to the adjoining hall. All of a sudden, every light in the museum turned on, and metal grates began to descend over every doorway and window. "We've been spotted," Caleb whispered as they ran. "We need to get out of here—now!"

They rounded a corner and nearly ran into a team of burly security guards, facing away from them, jogging briskly toward the hall that housed the *Mona Lisa*.

The super spies skidded to a halt, quieting their breathing until the guards turned another corner and disappeared from sight.

"I can guide you back to where you came in," said Sefu into their earpieces. "Hurry! There are guards everywhere! Take a left . . . now!" He paused for a second. "Oh, and move quietly, too!" He paused again. "And quickly! Quickly *and* quietly would be best."

"You're not helping, Sefu," Maddie whisper-shouted as her team ran back upstairs to the Egyptian collection. Searching the ceiling, she spotted the window with the hole in it and positioned herself below it, waving her arms to capture the practically invisible strands of nano-cord. She felt one, as thin as a hair, and grabbed it. "Over here!" she whispered. On her hip was a round spool and a crank.

"Wrap the filament around this, and you can wind yourself up using this crank-and-pulley system!" Maddie demonstrated, and started moving up just by turning the crank. She felt a surge of relief as it worked. "Thanks, Leonardo," she muttered under her breath, grateful that she'd stumbled over a similar design in one of his notebook sketches.

As they reeled themselves upward, a guard appeared. He spotted the spies and shouted, *"Arrêtez! Arrêtez!"* The kids cranked faster, still a few yards from the skylight.

"Hurry!" Sefu shouted in their earpieces. They reached the skylight and climbed through, just as more guards poured into the hall beneath them. The agents quickly put on their GeckoGrips and raced to the edge of the roof. Like a rock climber descending a mountain, Maddie bounced lightly with her toes against the building as she descended the nano-cord to ground level. *This would be fun*, she thought, *if we weren't about to get sent to French prison.*

The super spies scurried through the shadows and hid behind some bushes. Just then, spotlights clicked on, bathing the exterior of the Louvre in a blinding light, as police sirens filled the air.

"Run for it!" Lexi whisper-shouted.

The kids ran deeper into the shadows, back to where they had parked the scooters. The nearly silent scooters proved the perfect getaway vehicles, as the team raced down a road alongside the River Seine. They turned into

an alleyway just as a group of French gendarmes appeared,
searching with flashlights and walkie-talkies.

"That was close!" Lexi whispered.

Maddie's heart pounded as she guided her scooter down
the backstreets of Paris. When they'd returned their "bor-
rowed" scooters, and it was clear that no one had followed

them, her disappointment returned. "That was awful!" she cried.

"It's okay!" said Lexi. "We got away fine. We're okay."

"We just went off-mission to break into the world's most famous museum . . . and we left with nothing," said Maddie. She put her head in her hands.

"Then we should focus on next steps," said Caleb, putting his hand on Maddie's shoulder. "We can still find da Vinci's lost notebook. It's still out there somewhere."

"But we have precisely zero idea where!" said Maddie. "I don't even know what next steps we could take."

"So we had one bad night!" said Caleb. "Look around us! We're in the City of Light! Look over there!" He pointed behind Maddie at the outline of the Notre-Dame cathedral, lit up against the night sky. She looked up.

Paris really is beautiful, Maddie thought.

Suddenly, a screech in their earpieces made everyone jump.

"Help! We—" Doug's voice cut out.

"Doug? Are you okay?" Maddie called, suddenly guilty that they'd left Doug to watch over Chase all by himself.

"Get here as fast as you can!" Doug shouted. He sounded like he'd been crying. "There's been another accident!"

"We're on our way!" Lexi said.

Maddie, Caleb, and Lexi raced back into Le Zenith, where they saw Doug and Chase huddled together onstage, covered in soot. The air reeked of smoke, the disco ball was melted, and the stage floor was covered in black scorch marks. Doug was crying softy. Chase patted his back reassuringly, brushing bits of ash from Doug's shoulders as sprinklers in the ceiling dripped onto their heads.

"What happened?" Lexi asked as she rushed over to Chase and Doug.

"Are you all right?" Maddie asked, horrified. It looked like there had been some sort of explosion, which must have triggered the fire sprinklers.

"Does anything hurt? How's your breathing?" Lexi said, checking them for injuries. They'd all learned first aid and emergency response techniques at Camp Minerva.

"We're just a little . . . . startled," Doug said in a small voice.

"It was gnarly," Chase said, gesturing to the singed stage. "But I think we're okay."

"It's all my fault!" cried Doug.

"Not true, little man, not true," said Chase. "I blame myself."

"What happened?" asked Caleb.

"After the show, I read some of the reviews online," explained Chase. "Big mistake. Someone called my singing 'robotic.' Can you believe that?"

"Um . . . no," said Maddie, only halfway meaning it.

"It really hurt my feelings!" said Chase. "I couldn't rest knowing that someone had a less-than-life-changing experience at my show, so I asked Doug here for some feedback."

"It was awesome!" said Doug. "Chase hit the stage and he did the whole concert again, just for me!"

"I was showing Doug the routine for my next single, 'X-tra Credit,' 'cause I'm gonna sing it on the next leg of my tour," said Chase.

"And just as he hit the high note, the pyrotechnic machines went nuts!" said Doug. "They weren't even turned on! But they shot these huge streams of flames right at Chase!"

"It was freaky," Chase added. "We didn't get burned, but it was scary, you know? And Doug-man here jumped up and pushed me aside to block me from the flames. He saved me."

Doug's cheeks turned bright red and he stared down at his feet. "Just doing my job."

"Luckily, the sprinklers turned on in the nick of time," Chase said.

"Was anyone else around?" Caleb said as he examined the pyrotechnic machines for any signs of tampering.

"Nope—just us," said Chase. Maddie and Lexi exchanged worried looks. This was the first suspicious "accident" that had happened on their watch, and they hadn't been there.

"This is so not chill," Chase said. "We could've been toast. And my disco ball is ruined." He pouted.

Out of the corner of her eye, Maddie noticed a glinting reflection on the catwalk above the stage—*Is someone up there?*—but in the split second it took her to look up, the light had disappeared. She shook her head. *It was probably just the light bouncing off Chase's diamond wristwatch*, she thought.

She wanted to find out who did this so bad, she was seeing things!

Doug wiped the tears and bits of ash from his face, seeming to calm down a bit. "I've been feeling a little freaked out by this whole trip. I've never been out of the country before—and well, it's my tenth birthday in a few days. I've never been away from my family for a birthday before."

"Aw, Doug," Lexi said. "We'll be there for you!"

"Yeah, Doug," Maddie added. "Is there something special we can do to celebrate?"

Doug's face brightened slightly. "Well," he said, "since we're in Europe, I thought we could visit Ingolstadt, which is a city in Germany. A castle there is considered to be the birthplace of the Illuminati!"

Maddie smiled at the others. Typical Doug—always obsessed with the Illuminati.

"If it works out with the tour schedule, I mean," Doug said.

"I'm sure we can figure it out. Right, team?" Maddie said.

"Yeah!" said the others.

"Now that the party-planning sesh is over, did you guys find the notebook for the Future Predictor, at least?" Chase asked, looking intently at Caleb, Maddie, and Lexi.

Maddie hung her head. "No—we couldn't even get close

enough to the *Mona Lisa* to really look for the key."

"It was a bust," Lexi added.

"Are you kidding me?" Chase said, kicking a cloud of ash with his toe. "I'm in, like, serious danger over here!"

Maddie gulped. They'd have to find another way to locate the blueprints for da Vinci's future prediction device.

Or next time, Chase Chance might actually *be* toast.

CHAPTER 12

Prendere due piccioni con una fava.
Kill two pigeons with one fava bean.

The next morning, the Paris sky was gray, matching Maddie's mood after the previous night's failures and close calls. In the lobby of their fancy hotel, the super spies waited for Chase, who, as usual, was running ten minutes late. Finally, the pop star arrived and bounded over the group. "Wheels up for Madrid in twenty! *Besos!*"

"What?!" Maddie cried. She'd been so focused on getting to the bottom of the freak accidents and finding da Vinci's blueprints that she'd barely gotten any sleep. "I mean, I wish we had more time in Paris," she said in a friendlier tone.

Chase looked startled. He closed his eyes, took a deep

breath, and said calmly, "I can only perform at a hundred and ten percent when everyone's vibe is chill. CHILL!!!" he yelled. He took another long, slow breath. "I find chill vibes more conducive to my artistic growth, and on tour, everyone. Must. Be. Chill."

"Chill, totally," Maddie said, forcing a smile. Chase nodded, then went outside with a bodyguard to sign autographs for fans who'd slept overnight outside his hotel room.

The super spies hurried through the buffet line, loading up on croissants, fruit, and orange juice. "What are we gonna do now?" Maddie said, dejected, as they sat for a quick breakfast.

"I suppose we just keep following Chase on tour, right?" said Lexi.

"Maybe it's time to give up searching for da Vinci's lost notebook," said Maddie, with a sigh. "I really wanted to find it. I hoped it would help me—*us*, I mean—build the Future Predictor. But we have zero clues. And watching Chase is a full-time job."

"Shhh!" said Doug. "If he looks over here and notices we're not eating all red foods, he's going to freak."

"Yeah, he's kind of a . . . handful," said Lexi.

"Not much we can do about Chase," said Caleb. "Maybe we need to consider other ways of finding our bad guy."

Maddie nodded. At the moment, even she had to admit that the da Vinci lead was heading nowhere.

They quickly finished breakfast, hurried out to their

waiting limo, and were whisked to Orly Airport to board Chase's private plane. After a short flight, where they were served bowls of red pepper slices, raspberry smoothies, and more red M&M's, they landed in Spain.

They hopped on a luxury tour bus that wound its way through the city of Madrid. Maddie gazed out the window, but the sights failed to lift her spirits. They passed the Plaza Mayor, a large pedestrian square paved in cobblestones and surrounded by red-stone buildings, and Maddie could hear guitar music through the open bus window.

But being here in Spain just solidified that they were hundred of miles away from the *Mona Lisa* and her "key to the future"—and with it, the chances of finding the lost notebook. Maddie rested her chin on her hand, feeling frustration and sadness swirl together. If she was being completely honest, finding the future-prediction device was about more than just the mission for her. It was a chance to find out if her parents were in *her* future—not just her past. She wanted to know if they were really gone for good. Being back to square one felt lousy.

But just then, a banner hanging from a streetlight made her do a double take. It was an image of a woman—a painting—who looked strangely like . . . the *Mona Lisa*. What in the world? Why was a poster in Spain advertising a painting in Paris?

The words MUSEO NACIONAL DEL PRADO were

printed beneath the woman. "Hey, look!" Maddie elbowed Caleb and pointed.

"I don't understand . . . ," he said, furrowing his brow and tapping furiously on his S.M.A.R.T.W.A.T.C.H. After a moment, he shouted, "You guys! There's *another Mona Lisa!*"

"Are you kidding?" Lexi said. "I thought she was one of a kind!"

"Double the *Mona Lisa*s . . . ," Doug said, "double the mystery!" Lexi shot him a curious look. "That sounded cooler in my head," he admitted.

Maddie felt a rush of excitement and sat up straighter as she looked up the Prado Museum's opening hours. *Another* Mona Lisa. *What are the chances!* Maybe this one held the key to the future.

At the hotel, while Chase got a seaweed treatment at the spa, the team huddled in Maddie's room and did a safety analysis and risk assessment of Madrid.

"The concert doesn't start for a couple of hours," said Doug, who kept a laminated version of the tour schedule on him at all times.

"So we've got some time to check out the other *Mona Lisa* before the concert," said Maddie.

"You think when you look at this second *Mona Lisa*, you'll actually be able to tell what she's thinking?" asked Doug.

Maddie shrugged. "If you could tell what she was think-ing, it wouldn't be nearly as mesmerizing," she said. "Come on, we don't have any time to waste. Let's go see her!"

Caleb looked up from his *Global Nomad: Madrid* guide. "Yeah! And maybe we do some sightseeing on the way? This city is a cultural wonderland!"

"What did I just say about 'no time to waste'?" said Maddie, clearly in a rush.

"Appreciating other cultures is never a waste of time," said Caleb.

"Um, you guys? This is not a vacation. We have a mission to focus on," Lexi said. "And I don't think we should go off on our own again . . ."

Maddie knew what Lexi was about to say. She grimaced.

". . . without . . ."

Maddie really didn't want to hear Lexi's next word.

". . . Chase."

Maddie sighed. "Lexi's right," she said. "I hate to say this, but we've got to bring him with us. Our number one job is to protect him."

Maddie and her team got up and found Chase in the lobby, looking refreshed and relaxed from his spa treatment.

"Ooh," Caleb whispered, "hopefully he's more chill than before."

Despite the numerous acts of bravery the super spies had performed all over the globe, they were still nervous when approaching him. "Um . . . Chase?" asked Maddie. "Could we have a second?"

"Is it important?" asked Chase with a yawn.

"It's Level Three important," assured Caleb.

Chase stepped away from his conversation with his manager's manager and met the team in front of the hotel.

"So what's up?" the singer asked.

"We found another *Mona Lisa*," said Maddie. "Here. In Madrid. We want to scope it out . . . and even though you probably don't want to . . . and you can totally say no if you'd rather not . . ."

Chase raised an eyebrow.

Maddie continued. "We'd like you to come with us on the mission. And again, you can say no—"

"I'm in!" said Chase.

"You are?" asked Maddie. "I mean, of course you are. But . . . why exactly do you want to come with us?"

"I've always wanted to go on a mission! Being in the Illuminati Superstar Division is fun, but I never get to kick butt or look for clues or run headlong into danger. Dudes, I'm totally in!"

"Okay," said Maddie, surprised and pleased by Chase's enthusiasm. "We're going undercover as tourists. Let's change and meet back here in fifteen minutes."

Now dressed in Illuminati-issued tactical street clothes (aka big white sneakers, sunglasses, and baseball hats all made from burn-, rip-, and taser-proof materials), the group headed to the minivan. They piloted the invisible flying vehicle past elegant stone buildings, movie theaters, and restaurants on the Gran Vía. They parked in front of a huge white building lined with columns. It seemed to gleam in the bright sunlight against the cloudless blue sky.

They entered the museum, purchased tickets, and grabbed maps. Life was so much easier when they didn't have to sneak in.

Maddie whispered into her earpiece, "Sefu, what can you tell us about our location?"

"You've got cameras in the eastern corner of every room," he said, bringing up a hologram of the museum and zooming in on its security features. "You've also got guards. Two to a room."

"For now, we're just blending in," said Maddie.

"Just in case," said Sefu, "allow me to disable the proximity sensors near the second *Mona Lisa*. That way you can get extra close."

"Thanks, Sefu," whispered Maddie. "We're heading there now."

As they strolled through the marble hall, they saw masterpieces by Renaissance artists Raphael, Giovanni Battista Tiepolo, and Fra Angelico.

"Many of these artists . . . ," Doug whispered.

". . . were Illuminati, we know," whispered Lexi.

". . . were Illuminati," said Doug, finishing his thought.

Maddie turned in to a new gallery and gasped. *There really are two.* "There it is—another *Mona Lisa*!" she whisper-shouted to her teammates.

"That means . . . ," said Chase.

"That the search for da Vinci's secret notebook is still on!" said Maddie. "This painting could 'hold the key to the future'!"

"Come on," said Caleb, "let's get closer."

It hung in a thick wooden frame, with a little information plaque next to it. No thick glass covering it, no giant crowd-control barrier to keep them at a distance. This *Mona Lisa* was much more accessible than the one in Paris. They'd be able to walk right up to it! And that wasn't the only difference: the details of her robe, her face, and the landscape behind her were clearer.

"This one's just as beautiful," said Caleb.

"It's brighter, easier to see, especially without all the velvet ropes and glass," said Lexi. "But I still don't know what she's thinking."

"I like to think," said Chase, "that if the *Mona Lisa* were alive today, she'd be a Chase Chance fan."

Maddie rolled her eyes.

"Did you just roll your eyes at me?" asked Chase.

"No!" lied Maddie. "I was just . . . uh, looking around very, very quickly."

"Makes total sense," said Chase. "You field agents have the coolest skills!"

A small group of tourists with a tour guide walked by, gesturing at the painting.

"This work was thought to simply be a copy of the more

117

famous *Mona Lisa*, housed at the Louvre in Paris. But during restoration efforts, researchers realized that the all-black background was actually painted two hundred years later, *over* what had been there before."

Maddie leaned forward, intrigued. The guide held up a laminated photo of the exact same painting, but with a different, darker background. "This was what the painting looked like before restoration efforts." The guide pointed to the pale blues and mustard yellows in the background of the painting on the wall. "These vibrant colors were hidden underneath."

"So is this a real da Vinci?" a man from the tour group asked.

The guide smiled politely, having clearly been asked this question only a million times every day. "It depends what you consider 'a da Vinci.' Many consider this to be a true da Vinci. Most likely, it was painted by one of Leonardo's pupils in his workshop, but with some contributions or direction from Leonardo himself."

Maddie stared at this *Mona Lisa*. Even though there were differences from the one in Paris, the overall effect was similar. The regal yet peaceful expression on *La Gioconda*'s face, the elegance, the proportions, the overall effect of the painting itself—it all felt like a masterpiece. In this painting, her expression was more of a knowing smirk than a mysterious smile. Maddie liked it. It made *Mona Lisa* look like she was in on a really great joke.

As the tour group moved on, the super spies lingered in front of the *Mona Lisa*. There were laser sensors, but Sefu had disabled them. Up close, they could see much more detail and texture. Maddie felt a glimmer of hope. Maybe they'd find another clue leading them straight to da Vinci's lost notebook!

"I don't see anything that looks like a key," said Chase, sounding put-out.

"The tour guide gave me an idea," said Maddie. "Remember what she said about another painting under the surface?" She whipped out her supercharged hyperphone. "I have an infrared beam on this," she said. "Maybe we can use it to see if there's anything hidden underneath that the restoration missed. Leonardo may have painted more than meets the eye."

"Why didn't you think of this when we were at the Louvre?" said Lexi.

"I didn't know about under-paintings then!" said Maddie.

"Don't kick yourself," Caleb said. "Infrared doesn't work that well over glass."

Maddie smiled. "Let's scan the painting for anything that could be related to the 'key to the future' that Leonardo mentioned. Do you think one of you can distract the guard for a few minutes?" Maddie gestured with her head toward a woman in a uniform at the other end of the hall.

"Maybe I could pretend to be just some local nobody,

start to sing, and my amazing stage presence will draw people in," offered Chase. "'Who is this mysterious stranger with the golden voice?' they'll wonder."

"Yeah, I don't think so," said Maddie. "Lexi, any ideas?"

"Oh yeah," Lexi said. She tugged on Caleb's elbow. "How's your acting?"

"My performance as Nonspeaking Townsperson Number Three in my school production of *Our Town* was called 'riveting' . . . by my aunt Amelia," said Caleb as Lexi dragged him away.

Doug and Chase stood behind Maddie, helping to shield what she was doing from any passersby.

As Caleb and Lexi walked toward the guard, Lexi did her best impression of a spoiled brat. "I don't WANT to see more paintings. I WANT to go to the gift shop! Where are Mom and Dad?!"

"Yes . . . where are Mother and Father?" said Caleb, trying to play along, rather unconvincingly.

"I said, WHERE are MOM and DAD?" Lexi's voice boomed even louder as they reached the guard. "I think we're LOST!" She began to sob loudly.

The guard smiled kindly and said, "Can I help you, children?"

"PLEASE!" howled Lexi. "I want my MOMMY!"

"And Daddy, too, if we can track him down," said Caleb, a little startled by Lexi's tears, which looked very real. Her face was also becoming a unique shade of red, which contrasted alarmingly with her blue hair.

Meanwhile, Maddie quietly activated the infrared beam on her phone. She started at the top left-hand corner and adjusted the beam so that it illuminated a tiny circle on the face of the canvas. She moved it slowly left to right, as if she were "reading" the painting, working her way down inch by inch. In the distance, she could hear Lexi's wailing and footsteps retreating. Still, she'd probably have only a minute or two before another museumgoer came along.

Maddie gasped as a few stray lines appeared in her infrared beam, right beneath *La Gioconda*'s left hand, as if she were pointing to the spot. Markings that looked like letters appeared, in the dense, swirled writing that Maddie recognized from reading da Vinci's notebooks. *That's da Vinci's handwriting!* She read slowly. "Nit . . . na . . . ," she sounded out the first word. It didn't sound like anything Italian. Then she remembered—da Vinci wrote words backward, and in Italian. "Ro . . . mo—"

Suddenly, the sound of Lexi's voice echoed across the marble halls.

"I TOLD you they weren't at the gift shop!"

Maddie glanced over her shoulder, hiding her phone with her body. Apparently, Lexi and Caleb hadn't found their "missing" family and were headed back her way with the security guard. Maddie quickly snapped a photo with her phone, hoping it would capture the infrared message so she could study it later.

She spun around. "My dear sister and brother!" she shouted. "Mom and Dad just called. They're waiting for us by the café."

"See, Horatio?" Lexi asked, elbowing Caleb. "I told you that Clementina would find us."

"Yes . . . Horatio," Maddie said. "I'm so glad I found you and . . ."

"Off we go!" said Caleb. "Petronella and I are eager to catch up with Mom and Dad."

"Good. Let's go, Petronella. And thank you, ma'am, for your help," Maddie said to the guard. The guard opened her mouth to say something, but the three turned and walked quickly down the hall, followed by Chase and Doug.

After several twists and turns, the agents found an empty bench and sat down. As tourists streamed past them, they huddled together over Maddie's phone. She brought up the photo and zoomed in.

"Nit-na-rom-or . . . ," Lexi sounded out.

"I think this is da Vinci's mirror text," Maddie said. She grabbed a trusty pencil from behind her ear and started writing down the words in reverse order on her museum map:

DONDE EL REFLEJO DE LA LUZ DE LA LUNA
SE ENCUENTRA CON ROMORANTIN

"Where the moon's reflection of light meets romo-rantin," Caleb said. "It sort of makes sense. But what's 'romorantin'?"

"If I had to guess . . . ," said Lexi.

"You don't," answered Caleb.

"I'd say it's a type of lettuce," said Lexi.

Maddie pulled up the file on her da Vinci research and did a quick search on her hyper-phone. "Aha!" she said. "Romorantin!"

"Was I right?" asked Lexi.

"Not exactly," said Maddie. "Or at all. Sorry." She angled her phone so Lexi and Caleb could see. "Romorantin is a place—a city—where Leonardo made plans to design a new palace."

"Is that where the secret notebook is?" said Chase.

"Yeah, maybe at night, when the moonlight hits it, or something?" Lexi said.

Maddie frowned. She clicked from her notes to some of the articles where she'd done her research. "Actually, the project was never finished. It may have been the plague, or lack of money. So I don't think the answer is actually in Romorantin."

Caleb put his head in his hands. He was normally very

good at puzzles and liked being the first of the group to solve them. "Think!" he muttered to himself. "Think!"

Maddie thought back to her Illuminati training. All the code breaking, symbology, art history, geography, and animal-hypnosis courses she'd taken at Camp Minerva should have helped her in this moment. *Maybe not the animal hypnosis*, she thought. *That never worked that well.* Then she remembered something someone had told her. Was it Volkov? Archibald Archibald? No—it was her history teacher, Mr. Onderdonk. *When in doubt, ask for help.*

"Guys," said Maddie, "I need your help on this one."

"You know," said a voice in their ears, "just because I'm not there with you all doesn't mean I can't help." Sefu sounded a little irritated.

"Tell me you've got something," said Maddie excitedly.

They could hear Sefu tapping swiftly on a keyboard. He was quiet for a moment. "I've got it!" He sounded excited. "A codex including pages with da Vinci's plans for a palace at Romorantin is housed at the British Library," he said. "In London."

The super spies all looked at each other. Had they found another clue? Doug and Chase high-fived, and Maddie's heart leaped. They were getting closer to finding one of da Vinci's lost notebooks, which meant they were one step closer to finding a tool they could use to figure out who was targeting Chase Chance—and bring whoever it was to justice.

"Well, what are we waiting for?" said Chase. "Let's jet to London!"

"What about your show here in Madrid?" asked Caleb.

"Are you kidding?" asked Chase, grinning and popping his collar. "Postponing the show only makes the fans go even wilder. We'll change it from an afternoon show to a late-night show. I'll let my people know and they'll take care of it."

"You are so cool," said Doug, with a look of awe. And with that, the team ran back to their flying van.

Maddie readied the minivan by speaking a command into her S.M.A.R.T.W.A.T.C.H. "Set destination: London."

CHAPTER 13

Meglio tardi che mai
Better late than never

Minutes later, Maddie activated the invisibility shield as the flying minivan approached the London skyline. Caleb landed the minivan on the roof of St. Pancras train station, a huge redbrick building lined with arches and curved windows, with a tall clock tower at one end. Even though it was just a train station, the building looked like a palace. As Maddie scanned the foggy skyline, realizing she was now in the land of Shakespeare, Queen Elizabeth I, and the famous London Bridge, she felt like she had stepped back in time, impressed by the architecture and history of the city.

"We'll be fairly near the British Library here, and this

way we can keep the minivan out of the way," said Caleb. He, Maddie, Lexi, Doug, and Chase spilled out of the sliding door of the minivan into the drizzly London morning.

The group snuck down a utility staircase and reached ground level, where they made their way to the British Library. The library was an enormous building, redbrick like St. Pancras station but completely different in style— square and modern-looking, with panels of windows and angled gray roofs. The agents scurried across the brick courtyard and entered.

Inside, the building felt totally different. In the cavernous lobby, layers of windows and balconies drew their eyes upward to a soaring white ceiling. The thought of so many books and so much knowledge in one place was dazzling.

Caleb's eyes lit up. "I could spend all day—or all year— here!"

Maddie spoke into her hidden in-ear device. "Sefu, where's the notebook?" From HQ, Sefu traced a digital path through the blueprints and catalogue of the British Library, directing the others down several floors and through a labyrinthine path through bookshelves.

"Make a quick left and then your next right," said Sefu. He was watching the team live after hacking into the library's closed-circuit security cameras. He also made sure to loop the camera feeds so the security guards viewing the cameras would see old footage instead of the super spies snooping around.

"Ooh," said Caleb, "I don't suppose we have time to stop by the Wildlife and Environmental Sounds Collection."

"The what now?" said Maddie. "And also, no."

"They have copies of nearly every birdsong ever recorded!" said Caleb.

"In that case, we're definitely not stopping," said Maddie. "No offense to the birds."

"Don't get distracted," said Sefu. "Head down the staircase on your right, two more floors."

"How many floors down are we?" asked Lexi.

"The British Library has five basements," said Sefu. "And you're heading to the lowest one."

They exited the staircase. "Take one more right," said Sefu, "and you'll be there."

They reached a glass wall with a keypad by the door. "Just give me thirty seconds . . . ," Sefu said. Maddie could hear a keyboard clicking in the background as Sefu hacked into the British Library security system. After twenty seconds, there was a muffled click, and Lexi pushed open the door to the locked archives.

Inside, the air felt cool and dry and eerily silent. White metallic bookshelves and storage compartments stretched into the distance, seemingly endlessly.

Maddie pointed to a box of white cotton gloves. She put on a pair and gestured for her teammates to do the same.

Lexi put on a pair. "Ooh, call me 'Lady Lexi,'" she said in an exaggerated British accent.

"The gloves aren't to feel fancy," said Maddie. "They're to protect the books."

"The manuscripts here could be damaged by the oil on our skin!" explained Doug, the team's expert researcher. "Even the wrong levels of light or humidity or temperature could destroy them!"

They walked down one aisle, turned, and went down another aisle. Caleb's eyes nearly bugged out of his head when they passed a section housing Jane Austen's manuscripts. They walked past treasures like original Beatles song lyrics, an early illustrated edition of *Alice in Wonderland*, maps and diaries and scientific reports. Maddie wished they could stay and pore over each one. But if they were going to find a clue, they had to keep going.

"Guaranteed they put my lyrics in here one day," said Chase.

"I think you have to be British," said Doug. "And you're American."

"Actually, I'm Canadian, but I can see why you're confused. My marketing squad says I give off an 'all-American' vibe," said the pop star. Maddie ignored him and kept walking.

"You're just about there . . . three more feet," said Sefu.

A small sign said: *Arundel Codex.*

Underneath it was a large filing box. Maddie gingerly lifted the lid, and inside she found a collection of yellowy-brown manuscript pages. They were covered in

Leonardo's unique script, as well as drawings and diagrams, and seemed to be of different sizes.

"Is this the secret notebook we're looking for?" asked Chase. "I feel like the world's smartest explorer—if he could also dance really well."

"Sorry," said Maddie. "The Arundel Codex isn't the secret notebook, but I think da Vinci left a clue in it that will point us toward his secret writing."

"This book has info about . . . Rome something or other," said Lexi.

"Romorantin," said Caleb. "Da Vinci's never-built hideaway."

"There should be a whole section on Romorantin," Sefu said in Maddie's ear. She carefully lifted the pages, until she found ones with drawings of circles and squares arranged in a larger circle, enclosed in an octagon. Even though Maddie had seen hundreds of similar pages as digital reproductions, seeing da Vinci's writing in person was overwhelming.

"Leonardo himself actually touched these pages," said Maddie, in awe. "Can you believe it?" *It's like I'm shaking hands with a genius*, she thought.

"Get to work," said Sefu. "If someone finds you down there, you'll have a difficult time explaining how you got past the secure door."

"Good point," said Maddie. With Lexi's and Caleb's help, she began to pore over the notebook.

"Looks like the book is mostly plans for gardens and palaces," said Caleb.

"But what about the moonlight?" Lexi said. "There's stuff about rivers and people, but nothing about moonlight."

"Keep looking," Sefu said in their earpieces.

Maddie slowly paged through the codex as Lexi and Doug kept a lookout for any librarians, and Caleb held out his travel-sized magnifying glass as he helped Maddie look.

"Aha!" Maddie said, a little too loudly. "Here it is: Drawings and Notes on the Moon's Reflection of Light." She pointed a gloved finger to a page filled with writing, as well as diagrams of circles, lines, and angles.

"But where does this 'meet Romorantin'?" said Caleb. He stared at the page, and his face fell into his familiar *I'm figuring out a puzzle* expression: fingers rubbing his temples as his eyes darted every which way.

Maddie racked her brain, trying to think like Leonardo would.

"Maddie, can you take a picture of this page and the Romorantin pages?" Caleb said, his eyes looking straight ahead. She snapped the photos with her hyper-phone. "Send them to Sefu," Caleb continued. "I have an idea. Sefu, see if you can layer the images."

"Working on it," Sefu said. "Here, I'm sending you every permutation."

"I don't get it," Maddie said, reviewing the images. "I'm not seeing anything."

"Yet," said Caleb. "Maddie, didn't you say that da Vinci mirrored his writing?"

"He did," said Maddie.

"Hold up, fam!" said Chase. "What if he 'mirrored' his drawings, too?"

"Chase, that's brilliant!" Caleb said. "It's exactly what I was thinking, of course—but that's how I know it's brilliant!"

Maddie raised her eyebrows, surprised yet impressed. "Sefu, can you please flip the drawings, left to right, and transpose them again?"

Her phone beeped with a slew of new images from Sefu. She switched on the phone's holographic display so everyone could see them at the same time. Lines crisscrossed each other, creating clean, geometric shapes, mostly rectangles and squares, with a few circular sections, in a sort of X shape, with one side longer than the other.

"What the heck is that?" Lexi said, peering over Maddie's shoulder.

"Let me see!" Chase said, gently pushing Lexi aside. "Is it the blueprint for the device?"

"No . . . ," said Caleb, running his finger over the intersecting lines. "It's blueprints . . . for a building!"

Doug studied them. "A hundred and one feet high, two towers, thirty-two thousand square feet . . ."

"Wherever this building is, Leonardo must want us to go there!" said Maddie. "Maybe that's where he hid his secret notebook!"

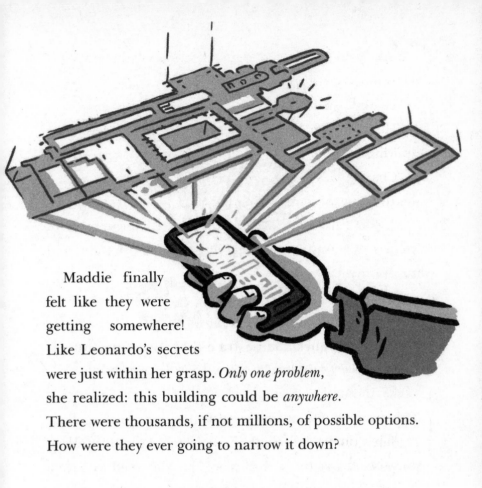

Maddie finally
felt like they were
getting somewhere!
Like Leonardo's secrets
were just within her grasp. *Only one problem*,
she realized: this building could be *anywhere*.
There were thousands, if not millions, of possible options.
How were they ever going to narrow it down?

CHAPTER 14

O mangi questa minestra o salti dalla finestra!
Either eat this soup or jump out of the window!

The group stared at the geometric design floating above Maddie's phone. The building was grand in scale and in purpose. It was the sort of place that deserved to have a piece of da Vinci's genius hidden somewhere inside it. The team wondered what kind of building would have this type of shape—and where it would be most likely to have been built.

"Hmmm . . . ," said Maddie, studying the design. "Sefu, can you cross-reference this design with blueprints for all European buildings?"

"Already on it," Sefu said, typing away.

"Why only European buildings?" Chase asked. "This

could be anywhere in the world."

"Because there are no records of da Vinci ever leaving Europe," Maddie said, remembering what she'd read in the biographies about da Vinci. "If Leonardo hid another clue, it was most likely on this continent!"

"Got it!" Sefu said. "I ran simultaneous searches on the proportions and angles of this design. I had to write a custom program in just a few seconds to analyze the parameters. . . ."

"Spit it out, dude!" said Chase.

"Well, I thought it was interesting . . . ," Sefu said, somewhat dejectedly.

"It is," Maddie said. "But aren't you the one always reminding us to move quickly?"

"Right," said Sefu. "It's a structure only a few miles from where you guys are right now."

"Would it be a church of some kind?" guessed Caleb. "That would make sense, given the time period and geographic location."

"Bingo," Sefu said. "It's the plans for Westminster Abbey."

Maddie had heard of that church. It was super-duper famous. And super-duper old.

"Neat-o!" said Doug. "Do you know how many Illuminati members are buried there?"

"I'm guessing a bajillion," said Lexi. "No! A bajillion and one."

"I'm cross-referencing these blueprints with the official blueprints from a British government database," said Sefu. "There's one difference: in da Vinci's drawing, there appears to be . . . an extra doorway inside the building!"

"A hidden door?" Maddie asked with visible excitement. "Let's go! Sefu, what's the best route there?"

As Sefu directed them, the team exited the British Library and hopped into the minivan. It drove itself through the London streets, filled with old-fashioned black cabs and red double-decker buses. It would be fun to explore this city as a tourist—without a mission . . . someday. She wondered if her parents had ever been to London. They'd been big travelers before she was born, and Maddie remembered that their house had been filled with souvenirs of their travels: wooden shoes called clogs from the Netherlands, hand-painted teapots from China, and colorful tiles from Portugal. *Maybe I could start collecting knickknacks to remind me of my travels*, Maddie thought. *Too bad every time I leave Philly, it's a secret!*

"Lexi," she asked, "do your parents travel much?"

"Oh yeah!" Lexi said. "We go to the state fair every year. Each of my brothers enters a cucumber into the Biggest Cuke contest. They win the gold, silver, and bronze every time, but my parents make all eight of them share the medals."

Maddie smiled. She liked hearing about Lexi's life. It was the exact opposite of hers in so many ways, but that didn't stop them from being friends.

Soon a massive building appeared, built from tan-colored stone, with dozens of spires poking up into the sky, which had turned blue, dotted with only a few fluffy clouds. Tourists lined the sidewalks, taking photos.

"Such a gorgeous day," Maddie said. "We really lucked out! I thought London was supposed to be rainy all the time."

As the approached the massive building, a huge clock tower loomed nearby, standing taller than the abbey and marking the time as nearly 4:00 p.m.

"Big Ben!" Caleb said, pointing to the clock tower. "Probably my favorite example of neo-Gothic architecture."

"Ben *is* big," said Chase approvingly. "I should get one of those for my backyard. Then I'd never run late again!" He stroked his chin. "Do you think they'd sell that one?"

"Sorry, Chase," said Maddie with a mischievous grin. "But maybe you could build an even bigger clock—and instead of chimes, it could play your songs."

Chase gazed at the towering timepiece. "Maddie," he said, shaking his head, "I never would've thought of that! That's why you're the genius of the group!"

The sunshine was so bright that Maddie and Lexi had to shade their eyes as they looked up at the soaring towers of Westminster Abbey, the tall windows and pointy spires that made them feel so tiny in comparison. Chase put on a pair of neon sunglasses and offered an extra pair to Doug. Caleb pulled a double-brimmed deerstalker hat from his backpack. The kind that Sherlock Holmes had made famous.

Lexi and Maddie looked at the hat, and then at each other, stifling a giggle.

"What? He's my hero, okay? And we're in London! Where else am I gonna get to wear this?" Caleb said defensively.

"I think it looks dope," said Chase, tossing Caleb an appreciative head nod.

They entered the abbey, pausing as their eyes adjusted from the bright sunlight outside to the dimmer, more reverent atmosphere inside. The ceilings soared overhead in graceful arches held up by giant stone columns. Maddie craned her neck, taking in the stunning architecture and the tall, pointed windows. She wondered what Leonardo would make of the elegant play of light and shadow, and what it would look like if he had painted this scene.

Maddie opened up the blueprint on her phone as Sefu guided them though their earpieces. They followed a tour guide and his tour to the other end of the abbey, then broke off and turned to the right, heading northwest, walking under colorful flags that hung partway up the towering walls.

The passed the scientists' corner, with a monument to Isaac Newton. *Got to remember to look him up in the Illuminati databases*, Maddie thought.

"There are so many Illuminati members buried here," whispered Doug.

"Newton?" asked Maddie.

"Yup," said Doug. "And Charles Darwin! And Stephen Hawking! Super scientists and super Illuminati."

"Charles Dickens is buried here, too," said Caleb. "I don't suppose he was—"

"Totally Illuminati," said Doug.

"Westminster Abbey is also where they hold all the British royal weddings," said Caleb.

"Did da Vinci design the building?" asked Lexi.

"No," said Caleb. "They started building it all the way back in the year 960, five hundred years before da Vinci was born."

"But da Vinci made an intricate drawing of the abbey in his notebook—plus that added door—so he could easily have left something here for someone to find," said Maddie.

They turned, entering the south transept.

"Look for a large, round window with intricate stained-glass designs," said Sefu.

"It's called a 'rose window,'" said Caleb. "We've got eyes on it." Sunlight filtered through the rose window, infusing the transept with a jewel-like glow.

The agents walked toward the window and stopped. Maddie looked around. A skinny wooden door sat flush with the stone wall.

"Is this the spot?" Chase said, reaching toward the door.

"Gotta be," said Maddie. "Try it."

Chase glanced around at the tourists, praying or walking around with their heads tilted back, taking photos of the majestic cathedral. He twisted the knob and nudged the door. Nothing.

"Step aside." Lexi put her hand on Chase's shoulder. "This is kinda my specialty," she said, moving forward. She gave the wooden door a hard shove with her shoulder, and it popped open.

The group raced through the door and shut it behind them, hoping no one noticed. They found themselves in a wood-paneled hallway, leading left and right, with another door in front of them.

"There should be a stairway right there, I think," Sefu's voice said in their earpieces.

Caleb tried the door in front of them, and it opened into a tiny, cylindrical space with a wooden spiral staircase. He led the way, clinging with one hand to a central pole from which wooden stairs radiated out like spokes. There was no railing. It smelled musty, like old wood and old stone, and Maddie sneezed as they made their way higher and higher.

"This is pretty good cardio. Right, my dude?" Chase said, clapping Doug on the back. Doug nodded, breathing too heavily to say anything.

"We must be inside one of the spires," Caleb said, huffing

and puffing. "I wonder how far up we have to go."

"I can carry you if you're tired," said Lexi brightly. "This is nothing compared to running up the pyramids at Camp Minerva."

"You know I don't like being picked up," Caleb said sternly. "I just like to know where we're going."

On and on they climbed. They reached a landing at the top of the stairs and took a moment to catch their breath. All of them, even Lexi, were covered with a thin sheen of sweat. *Where is Leonardo leading us?* Maddie thought as her leg muscles burned. She peered out of a carved stone window and looked down. They were so high up. The people beneath them looked so tiny. Maddie felt momentarily dizzy. They must be hundreds of feet high.

"Now what?" she asked, looking around the landing for any sort of da Vinci-esque clue or sign in the stone walls. *Is this where da Vinci hid his secret notebook? There has to be something here*, Maddie thought. *After all, Leonardo practically drew us a map!*

"I don't know," Sefu said. "This is where the trail stops."

"Man, if this is another dead end, then I'm totally not going to feel chill," Chase said. "And we'll be no closer to figuring out who the bad guys after me are."

Caleb ran his fingers lightly over the walls, and Lexi pushed on them, trying to find a loose panel or secret passageway. All of a sudden, adult voices echoed far beneath them. Maddie held a finger to her lips.

"Someone must have seen us come in and alerted security," she whispered. "We have to hurry!" The super spies redoubled their efforts, checking the walls and corners and even the ceiling for any hint of a clue. Maddie ran her hands over the wooden floor.

"Maybe we're in the wrong place," Lexi said. "There's nothing here!"

Just then, Maddie felt an almost-imperceptible difference in one of the floorboards. It could have been warped with age, but she tried pressing on it anyway.

The voices grew louder as several guards made their way up the long spiral staircase.

"Hurry!" Caleb whispered. "I won't be able to think of a good cover story if we get caught! I used all my acting skills back in Madrid!"

Maddie gave up pushing on the floorboard and tried pulling. That didn't work either. Finally she tried pushing down on one end and motioned for Lexi to pull on the other. The floorboard swung upward, revealing a tiny brass handle in the layer underneath. Maddie pulled on the handle, opening a section of the floor.

"A trapdoor!" Her pulse quickened. Da Vinci's map had led them right here. This was it, Maddie could feel it.

"Let's hustle, fam!" Chase urged.

"Oi, who's up there?" a male voice shouted.

Maddie opened the trapdoor all the way and pulled out a small brown notebook. She nearly screamed.

The secret notebook!

Maddie was dying to peek inside to see what it contained. She wished they still had their white cotton gloves from the British Library. After all, this notebook was an artifact, hundreds of years old. Maddie carefully tucked the book into her backpack as the huffing and puffing of several security guards echoed up the stone tower. They had to get out of there.

"Wait—what's this?" Lexi said, pulling out some sort of fabric that had been folded underneath the notebook. She carefully shook it out, releasing a huge cloud of dust. Four large triangular panels made a sort of pyramid, lined with a thin wooden frame. Ropes descended from the corners. Something tickled in the back of Maddie's brain—there was something familiar about this. She tied the ropes together into a strongest knot she could remember from her knot-tying course at Camp Minerva.

"I've seen this before!" said Maddie. "Lexi, open the window!"

Lexi pushed open the heavy window.

"Do you all trust me?" Maddie said, tying the rope around everyone's waist.

They all spoke at the same time. "Yes!" said Caleb and Lexi.

"Maybe," said Doug.

"Not really," said Chase.

Just then, four black hats and ruddy faces popped into view. The men breathed heavily, and were certainly not amused to find five agents at the top of the stairs, wrapping themselves in rope.

"What're you doing?" asked the lead officer.

"A research project?" Maddie said, with a nervous laugh.

As the security guards reached the landing, she yanked the others to the window. "If you don't trust me, then trust in the genius of da Vinci!" she whispered.

And before she had a moment to second-guess her decision, she jumped.

CHAPTER 15

Rosso di sera bel tempo si spera.
When the sky is red at night, good weather is hoped for.

Maddie felt her stomach drop—this was worse than any amusement park ride she'd ever been on. And way scarier than rappelling down the side of the Louvre. They all screamed. Suddenly, she felt a lurch in her midsection as the rope tightened around the five falling super spies. Maddie looked up, seeing the pyramid-shaped parachute now filled with air. The shocked faces of the guards peered down at them from the window as they descended.

"Ha!" Maddie yelled. "It worked!"

"You mean, there was a chance it wouldn't work?" gasped Caleb.

"Wheee!" Lexi yelled as Doug whimpered softly.

"I was pretty sure it would work," Maddie said as they glided gently down, down, down. "I recognized this design from Leonardo's sketches. But I never knew that he built a prototype!"

As the agents floated closer to the crowd, they noticed people pointing at them, aiming cameras and phones in their direction.

"What are we gonna do?" Chase said. "It's like the paparazzi down there! These pictures are going to be all over the internet—and this is *not* my most flattering angle."

"We have bigger things to worry about," Maddie said, as the ground seemed to rush up to them alarmingly fast. "Brace for impact!"

The agents landed on a patch of grass, rolling to break their fall, which was a little challenging, since the five of them were tied together with rope.

"Ow!" said Lexi, landing at the bottom of the pile.

"Ow!" said Maddie as their momentum rolled her to the bottom of the pile.

"OUCH!" yelled Caleb. They rolled to a stop, with him squished at the bottom.

"Oof!" Doug and Chase shouted at the same time.

The parachute landed gently on top of them, covering them in a fabric pyramid, hiding them from view.

"Are you all okay?" asked Maddie, feeling her arms and ribs for broken bones. Everything hurt, but she hoped she was just bruised.

"I'm feeling a little pickled," Lexi said, rubbing her head and blinking her eyes. One of her cheeks was smudged with dirt.

"I'm feeling a lot pickled," said Doug, picking himself up. "But nothing I can't handle."

"As long as I didn't damage this priceless face, I'm good," Chase said, shaking his bangs back into their trademark swoop over his piercing eyes. Apparently, he had lost his sunglasses in the fall.

"Please get off me!" said Caleb.

"Sorry, Caleb," Maddie said, sliding off him. His Sherlock hat had fallen off, and she placed it gently back on his head and dusted the dirt from his shoulders. "Are you all right?"

"I think so. The parachute slowed our momentum just enough. But we could have died!" Caleb sounded more shaken than angry.

"We didn't, though! I knew Leonardo's invention was sound!" Maddie marveled that a contraption built hundreds of years ago by Leonardo's hands had saved them. If she had had more time to think about it, she might not have tried it out for the first time from such a great height. She quickly untied them from the ropes.

A woman in a sundress appeared, clutching a tiny Pomeranian, which was wearing a matching sundress. "Are you kids hurt?" she asked in a singsongy British accent, but with a concerned look on her face. When she noticed

Chase, her eyes bulged in recognition. "Are you . . . . ?"

"We're fine, thank you!" Lexi yelled as they got to their feet and ran headlong into the crowd of bystanders.

The agents scattered in the crowd, ducking and rolling. Lexi snatched a big, floppy hat from someone's hand and yanked it on for a temporary disguise. Maddie turned her sweatshirt inside out so that it looked gray instead of green.

Sefu's voice crackled in their earpieces. "Hello? Hello? What's happening? Do you read me?"

"Yes," Maddie gasped as she hid behind a cart selling mini replicas of Big Ben and the Union Jack flag. "We had to, um, disappear in the crowd. We kinda made a bit of a scene. . . ."

"Well, zigzag, zigzag!" Sefu said.

"I'm zigging!" Lexi said in Maddie's ear-comm.

"I'm zagging!" Caleb said at the exact same time.

Maddie whirled around, trying to spot them. She saw Caleb ducking behind a park bench, and Lexi in her ridiculously big hat, peeking around a red telephone booth. Chase took the sunglasses off Doug's face and put them on his own to try and blend in.

Maddie whispered directions into her earpiece, and the group met at the phone booth. They squeezed inside.

"I think we're safe, at least for a while," Caleb said. "But we've got to get our minivan and get back to Madrid for tonight's concert!"

"Right," said Maddie. "And besides, we got what we came for: da Vinci's notebook."

She checked her backpack, making sure that the fragile notebook hadn't been smashed by their fall. It seemed to be in one piece, thank goodness. She wanted to page through it right then and there, but she knew they'd have to get somewhere safe and private first. A whole crowd of people had just seen them jump off a church spire. A very famous church spire.

"How are we going to get out of here?" asked Lexi.

Their minivan appeared around a corner. "Your chariot awaits," said Sefu, who was remote-driving the van from Camp Minerva. The van gave its signature *beep-BEEP-beep* to let them know it was there.

"C'mon, fam, we're almost there! All you need is a little X-tra cred-it to make it *throooooogh*," Chase sang. He picked Doug up and carried him piggyback style. "You know that I got yoooooouuuuuu."

"Sing it, Chase!" said Maddie, feeling giddy. Not only were they doing their duty—keeping Chase safe—they had just found a notebook that Maddie believed was full of inventions that could solve all their problems. "This is what a successful mission feels like!" she said.

Then the hairs on her arms stood straight up. *I must be really excited*, Maddie thought, until she noticed the hair on Chase's head start to fly out of place. *Wait . . . is the air filling with static electricity?*

Suddenly, a huge beam of light crackled down, striking the ground just feet away from Maddie. "Whoa!" she screamed. Before she could catch her breath, a loud clap of thunder burst right over their heads.

Caleb and Lexi screamed. "What's going on?"

Chase ducked in fear. Doug fell on his back with a thud. The air smelled like burnt wires.

"Yikes!" yelled Lexi. "Was that . . . ?"

"A bolt of lightning!" Maddie said, practically hyperventilating.

Caleb looked up at the sky. "But it's not raining! There are no storm clouds! This doesn't add up."

"That weird stuff is happening again!" yelled Chase. "Run!"

"Let's get to the van," Maddie said. "Come on!"

Another bolt of lightning hurtled down, striking just a few feet away from Lexi.

"AAAHHHH!!!" she yelled.

Terrified tourists ran in every direction, trying to find shelter. Families huddled together under shop awnings. Even the birds seemed to be in a panic, flying every which way.

The super spies ran as fast as they could, veering to the right. Another bolt struck, this time right behind Chase and Doug. The team froze, not knowing where the next bolt would strike. The pedestrians nearby simply screamed.

Maddie got the horrifying feeling that someone on the

ground was watching her. She scanned the crowds. A girl her own age with long black hair and sharp black eyebrows stood alone amid the panic, making no attempt to run or hide. She smiled at Maddie, and then stepped backward, disappearing into the crowd.

"Did anyone else see . . . ?" Maddie started to ask when another bolt landed just inches away from Chase.

"It's like the lightning is targeting us directly!" said Caleb.

"It's targeting Chase!" said Maddie. "Sefu, open the doors!"

The minivan doors slid open, but it was still several yards away. Maddie knew the next strike would hit Chase if she didn't think fast. She pulled out her hyper-phone.

"I want you guys to run for it," Maddie said. She grabbed Chase's arm. "But you stay here."

She unscrewed the back of her hyper-phone and removed the air ionizer she'd added. "Lightning happens when the air becomes ionized," she mumbled, fiddling with her ionizer's wires and reversing its energy flow. "If we can deionize the air, the lightning won't be able to form!" She mounted her now-reverse-engineered deionizer back into her phone, screwed it together again, and tossed it to Chase.

I hope this works, she said to herself.

"What do I do with this?" asked a freaking-out Chase.

"Hold it above your head . . . NOW!" shouted Maddie.

Chase lifted the phone above his famous coif. Another

bolt of lightning shot from the sky directly above him. Maddie watched it happen in slow motion: just as the bolt was inches from Chase's head, her deionizer kicked in, and the lightning bolt fizzled out, losing its shape as its energy dissipated harmlessly into the air.

"I knew that would work!" lied Maddie. "Come on, let's run for it!"

They broke toward the van. Her friends were already inside, and she and Chase dove in and shut the door. "Let's go!"

As the van lurched into the sky and sped southwest toward Spain, Maddie hunched over with her head in her lap.

"That was amazing, Maddie!" Lexi said.

"You saved Chase! But you could've been killed!" scolded Caleb.

Maddie just sighed.

"Your invention worked!" said Doug. "That was awesome!"

"Thanks . . . but those bolts of lightning . . . they were so close to us," said Maddie. "Way too close to be coincidence."

"It's like wherever I moved, the lightning bolts moved with me," said Chase, still in shock.

"Whoever is targeting Chase is really powerful," said Lexi.

"That type of technology," said Sefu over the van's speakers, "means we are likely up against another master inventor."

"I'd almost think it was Zander Lyon," said Maddie, forcing herself to laugh.

"Impossible," said Caleb.

"You sent him flying over the Hudson River, Maddie," Lexi reminded them. "He's gone."

"But whoever is after Chase is just as smart. And just as determined," said Sefu.

"You're right," said Maddie, taking da Vinci's lost notebook from her bag. "Using this, we can build the future prediction device. It's our only chance of keeping Chase—and us—safe."

CHAPTER 16

Chi troppo vuole nulla stringe.
Grasp all, lose all.

Maddie carefully opened the brown leather-bound notebook and began gently turning the brittle pages. Again, she wished she had those white gloves from the British Library.

Caleb gulped. "Maddie, are there plans in the notebook?"

Maddie started reading lines and lines of da Vinci's unique mirror script. She whipped out her hyper-phone, opening the camera function and translation apps to make sense of the pages written in Renaissance Italian.

"These are notes," said Maddie, "from before he began to design the Future Predictor. Look, he made a list of pros and cons of building it!"

"'Pro,'" said Caleb, reading off Maddie's phone. "'Could

154

prevent unnecessary deaths from disasters.'"

"'Con,'" read Lexi. "'Unscrupulous profit-chasers could gain riches from exploiting the future.'"

"Look down here," Maddie said. She read da Vinci's writing aloud: "'Is the future stable? Or is it forever in flux? If one could learn the future, could one change it?'"

"That's some thoughtful stuff," said Chase.

"Agreed," said Maddie. "Looks like Leonardo knew what he was getting into." She pointed to the bottom of the page. "'I cannot let such a marvel fall into the wrong hands,'" she read. She shuddered, thinking about how awful it would be if someone with evil intentions had the power to predict the future. If Zander Lyon had such a device, he would've easily thwarted anyone who tried to stop him from taking over the world. She sure hoped that they could find da Vinci's secret blueprints before anyone evil did.

Maddie paged through the notebook as they flew. "Da Vinci sure wrote a lot about the ethics of predicting the future," she said. She was getting anxious. "But I don't see any design drawings or schematics that would actually help us build a future-prediction machine."

Chase leaned over Maddie as she carefully leafed through the pages. In addition to the lines of mirror text and plenty of drawings, there were sketches of what looked like clouds, rain, even a swirling hurricane. There were outlines for something that looked like an elongated wind-mill, something that looked like a rudimentary camera lens, and other strange and bewildering contraptions. Maddie wondered what they all did. It would take ages to pore through the notations and diagrams. She continued to flip the pages—she had no idea what a future prediction-device looked like, but she'd keep looking until she found it.

"Have you found it yet?" Chase asked, peering over her shoulder.

"Not yet. Keep your eyes peeled for words like *futuro* and *previsione*," Maddie said, writing the words backward on a scrap of paper so that the others could see what they would look like on the page.

But there was something different about the writing in this notebook. The letters looked the same, but still, something felt off. She couldn't put her finger on what. Maddie turned toward the back of the notebook, skimming for anything that seemed to hint at a future-prediction device.

"Have you found it yet?" Chase asked again.

"I'm going as fast as I can!" Maddie said, exasperated. "I know you're freaked out by what happened, but there are hundreds of pages here!"

"Chase, are you okay?" said Lexi. "You don't seem very . . . chill."

"You don't have to read every single page," Chase said. "Just find the device!" He grabbed the notebook and started pawing through the fragile pages.

Just then, the minivan shuddered slightly.

"Hey!" Maddie couldn't let this priceless artifact, so integral to their mission, get damaged by a pop star, even if he was technically Illuminati. She snatched it back.

"Whoa, whoa, chill," said Chase. "Why are you messing with my vibe?" He grabbed the notebook out of Maddie's hands—again—moving his finger down each page as if he were speed-reading. The others watched warily, not sure what to make of this power struggle.

"Give. That. Back!" Maddie said, and lunged for the notebook. The others stared at Maddie and Chase, flicking their eyes from one to the other, as if they were watching a tennis match.

Maddie grabbed hold of one end of the notebook as the minivan lurched again in the other direction, causing everyone to jerk the other way, stopped only by their tightened seat belts. Chase and Maddie both gripped the notebook, unwilling to let go.

"You guys, stop it!" cried Doug. "I hate confrontation!"

"Can one of you help me?" Maddie yelled. She stumbled toward the front of the minivan as it dipped and banked in the air.

Sefu's voice came through the minivan's speakers. "Alert, agents. You are encountering a sudden windstorm. Make sure your seat belts are fastened. I'm going to navigate through this."

But Chase unbuckled his seat belt to get another hand on the notebook. "Just let me have it," he whined.

"No," Maddie said. She could not trust Chase with this precious notebook—not after all they'd done to find it. She could not let him risk destroying the precious knowledge inside it—and her hopes of what they could do with it.

"I. Just. Want. To. Find. The. FUTURE PREDICTOR!" Chase yelled, finally prying the notebook from Maddie's desperate grasp, leaving her clutching only a single page. But he fell backward against the wall of the minivan, jostling the sliding door. The door flew open, and Chase screamed, clawing to hang on to the nearby seats. Air whooshed out of the cabin, sucking loose M&M's, magazines, hats, and anything that wasn't secured right out into the open air.

Including the notebook.

"NOOOOOOooooooo!" Maddie cried out as da Vinci's notebook flew out of Chase's hands and spiraled into the clouds. She felt a surge of rage, sadness, and disbelief as it fell out of view. Chase hoisted himself into a bucket seat as the emergency lights started flashing. Maddie glared at him. The lost notebook was lost—*again*. And it was

THE LOST NOTEBOOK!

all Chase's fault. And maybe a little bit hers. But mostly his.

"You're losing altitude quickly," warned Sefu over the van's speakers. "The vehicle isn't responding to my commands. I'm enabling manual control. Maddie, take the wheel!"

Maddie closed the open van door then switched places with Doug, who was in the driver's seat. She pulled up desperately on the wheel as the minivan descended sharply. "Get ready for a rocky landing!" she shouted. She counted down, "Three . . . two . . . ," but the flying van slammed into the ground of a farmer's field before she could finish.

Maddie blinked and looked around the crashed vehicle. Her friends were battered but uninjured thanks to the van's high-tech, ultra-shock-absorbent airbags. But da Vinci's priceless, secret notebook was now gone forever.

Chi trova un amico, trova un tesoro.
He who finds a friend, finds a treasure.

Maddie dug her hands into the armrest and shut her eyes. Hot tears leaked out. She should've talked to Chase, persuaded him to give the notebook back. She should have been more careful. She should have waited until they landed to look through the notebook. Not only had she put the whole team in danger with her reckless actions, their best chance at building the future-prediction device was gone for good.

"Everyone okay?" asked Lexi as she kicked the stuck van door open. The spies climbed out of the minivan into the field they had crashed in.

"Everyone's vitals are normal," said Sefu, monitoring

the sensors woven into every piece of Illuminati clothing. "No broken bones. Just some elevated heart rates."

"That would be me," said Caleb, hunched over and catching his breath. "But I'll be fine in a minute."

"I have strange news," said Sefu.

"I think I already know," said Maddie. "The windstorm that blew us off track mysteriously dissipated right after we crashed."

"Exactly," said Sefu.

"Which means," said Caleb, "that whoever is after Chase hasn't given up yet."

Maddie was tired and bruised, but she knew they couldn't stay in that random field for the rest of their lives. "Let's start fixing the van," she said.

They all got out of the van, and as Maddie opened the hood of the vehicle, smoke billowed from the engine.

"We have some fixin' to do," Lexi said quietly.

Maddie nodded as she got to work. She tried to keep tears from spilling out of her eyes. The notebook was gone—and with it, any chance of finding the Future Predictor, or finding out if she'd ever see her parents again. She wasn't the only one crying. Doug sniffled, his eyes red and swollen.

"Hey, buddy," Lexi said, putting her arm around Doug. "Don't cry. We'll figure out the next clue somehow!"

Doug looked up, tears pouring down his face. "It's not about the stupid clue. It's my *birthday*!" His little shoulders shook with sobs. "And no one remembered!"

Maddie's mouth went dry, and Caleb and Lexi stared at her in horror. They were supposed to have done something special for Doug's birthday. After all, this was his very first birthday away from home. He was the youngest member of their team, and it was obvious he was a little homesick, even though he tried to hide it. They'd all been so wrapped up in their search for this missing notebook, they'd completely forgotten to make any plans for Doug.

"We were going to go to Ingolstadt, remember? And visit the birthplace of the Illuminati?" Doug looked at his feet. "We just talked about it yesterday!"

Maddie barely remembered that conversation. She'd been so focused on finding the notebook, following the clues—with the hopes of maybe finding out some scrap of information about her parents. Clearly, Lexi and Caleb had also forgotten all about it in the danger of a mission filled with lightning strikes, windstorms, and a disco-ball explosion.

"Doug, I'm so sorry," Maddie said, feeling like the worst friend in the world. "I don't know how we can ever make it up to you!"

The team was silent for a moment, all feeling guilty.

"I know how!" Chase said, with a twinkle in his eye. "Is the van fixed yet?"

"Sort of," said Maddie. "Not exactly as good as new. But good enough. It can fly but it can't drive, oddly enough."

"Then let's jet!" said Chase, hustling the team into the van.

He tapped a few messages into his phone as the minivan took off. "Sefu, my main man," said Chase, "will you do us the honor of rerouting our flight?"

"Where to?" asked Sefu over the comms.

"We're going to Ibiza!" Chase said.

"What's E-beeth-a?" said Doug dubiously. "Is it more exciting than Ingolstadt?"

"Way more exciting than some drafty old castle! I've got a mansion there, and it's going to be so lit when we land!" Chase said, doing a quick pop-and-lock motion with his arms.

Doug looked skeptical, but it was hard not to catch Chase's enthusiasm as he asked Doug what his favorite ice cream flavor was, his favorite color, his favorite candy, and a bunch of other random questions. Then Chase commandeered the entire back row of seats to use "as an office," and made some calls too quietly for the others to hear.

Maddie exchanged glances with the others as the van banked steeply to change course. What was Chase up to? And would it be enough to make it up to Doug? Maddie felt terrible that they'd forgotten Doug's birthday. She'd had three birthdays now without her parents, and even though Jessica and Jay did their best to make them special, baking her favorite cake (Funfetti with neon-green icing) and singing "Happy Birthday," birthdays were just another reminder of how long her parents had been missing. So they weren't really days she looked forward to, or paid much attention to anymore.

The minivan descended over turquoise waters and landed on a private airstrip. It was hot and sunny on the tarmac, and the tropical breeze felt good on Maddie's skin. Chase waved the super spies over to a waiting banana-yellow stretch SUV, with Chase's face airbrushed on the hood. Lexi rolled her eyes, but Doug started bouncing lightly on the balls of his feet. Maddie smiled to herself. She knew that meant that Doug was getting excited. She hoped he wouldn't be disappointed.

"I've got some Illuminati engineers on call," said Chase. "They can fix the van, then they'll have it fly over to my place. Let's roll!"

The SUV drove past palm trees, hotels, and buildings with bright white walls and red roofs, until finally they came to a tall wooden privacy gate with interlocking gold *C*s carved in the center. Chase pressed a button on his phone and the gate swung outward, revealing a perfectly manicured emerald-green lawn covered in colorful shapes.

The super spies rolled down their windows as the SUV rolled up the driveway, and Doug's jaw dropped. There were bouncy houses in the shape of castles in every color— Maddie counted at least ten—and a mini carousel (which played Chase's latest album as it rotated), and llamas and peacocks strolled the grounds.

"Whoa. This is awesome!" said Doug, nearly falling out of the SUV window as he leaned out to take it all in.

"Hang on, little buddy," said Chase. "Wait till you see what's out back."

They hopped out of the car, and a butler handed each of them a pair of sunglasses, a floppy sun hat, a party blower, and a gift bag filled with thousands of dollars' worth of skin-care products, Chase Chance–branded hot sauce, bubblegum, and kombucha, and a signed copy of Chase's new a cappella album, with each part sung by him. "Um, thank you?" said Maddie, wondering what the heck she'd do with all this stuff.

Doug peered up from his slightly-too-large hat at Chase's house, which had been decorated with balloons and streamers in Doug's favorite color, sky blue. "Your house is the same color as your SUV!" said Doug, grinning.

"It's a custom color," said Chase. "They call it Chase Yellow, and I own the exclusive rights to it."

"You own the rights to a color?" asked Maddie. "That's actually . . . kinda cool."

Lexi blew her party blower, making a loud squawk, and though Caleb covered his ears, he laughed. Maddie felt her shoulders relax a bit. *Maybe this little detour and celebration is just what Doug needed to cheer up.* She watched her best friends, and her new friend, Chase, run through Chase's lawn sprinklers, splashing each other. *Maybe this is what we* all *needed.*

She was still mad at Chase, but she tried to be cheerful for Doug's sake. You only turn ten once, after all, and they all wanted him to have a great day.

Doug ran up to one of the llamas, which snorted loudly, spit profusely, and turned away from the young Illuminati agent. "I don't think this one likes me very much," said Doug.

Chase led the super spies through his mansion, furnished in comfy beanbag chairs and massive white couches. "I never sit on the couches," said Chase. "I'm way too scared of getting them dirty!"

Chase turned toward the backyard and pointed out giant pop-art portraits of himself hanging on the walls. "These are made by a street artist named Mr. Flimflam. I'm pretty sure he's making fun of me, but I like them anyway."

Finally, Chase led them outside. Maddie's jaw dropped when she saw what Chase had laid out for them. There was a popcorn machine, a cotton-candy machine, an ice cream sundae station, an add-your-own-toppings pizza table, and much more.

"Mini hot dogs!" said Caleb, noticing a tray of tiny, sizzling treats along with a rainbow of dipping sauces.

"Mini cheeseburgers!" said Lexi.

"Mini chicken nuggets!" said Maddie.

"Eating miniature food is good for your metabolism," said Chase. "Plus, they make you feel big, which is fun."

"I feel like a giant," said Doug, stuffing two mini-dogs into his mouth.

Chase turned a corner, then peeked back at the super spies. "Guys, I want you to check out the best part of the house: the pool."

They ran over to Chase. Behind him glistened a huge swimming pool with three waterslides of various heights. Doug's eyes grew huge, and he almost knocked Chase over as he jumped up to give him a hug.

"This. Is. So. AWESOME!" he yelled.

"I told you it'd be epic," Chase said, ruffling Doug's hair.

"It's great to have real friends to share this with. Speaking of friends, I believe you know . . ."

Everyone turned to see Sefu walking across the backyard.

"Sefu!" cried Maddie. Their friend had flown in just for Doug's birthday.

"Apologies if I act a bit tired," said Sefu. "But I'm a little jet-lagged. Or, rather, flying-minivan-lagged," he added, with a sheepish smile. Maddie laughed extra hard, since she was pretty sure that was the first joke Sefu had ever made.

Sefu took Maddie aside. "I'm sorry to hear about the lost da Vinci notebook," he said.

"Not much we can do now," said Maddie. "What do you think Dewey the Hologram Librarian would do if she knew we found and then lost da Vinci's book?"

"The information would prove so overwhelming to her AI routines that she would go mad and trap us underground with her forever," said Sefu.

Maddie laughed.

"That was not a joke," said Sefu.

"Come on, guys!" yelled Chase. "It's pool time!"

The super spies changed into bathing suits provided by Chase, and Lexi cannonballed into the deep end of the pool, soaking Caleb, who had been easing himself down the ladder, trying not to get his glasses wet. Sefu did a backflip into the water. Chase had given Doug sky-blue water wings, goggles, and a noseclip ("I'm not the strongest swimmer," Doug had admitted shyly), and then Maddie, Chase, and Doug went down the three waterslides at the same time, splashing into the pool.

After they'd swum, they sat around in outdoor beanbag chairs, eating birthday cake with sky-blue icing. A peacock wandered over, stealing a crumb from Lexi's plate.

"This is the best birthday I've ever had!" mumbled Doug, his mouth full of cake.

"So you're not mad at us anymore?" said Lexi.

"No way!" said Doug. "This is way better than breaking into some old German castle. Who knew you could rent so many bouncy houses?"

"Yeah," whispered Maddie, leaning over to Chase. "How'd you pull this off, on such short notice?"

"Oh, it's always set up like this," Chase said. "I just called my staff to switch out the colors of the decorations and the type of cake, and to put out Doug's favorite foods. You gotta be ready to party at a moment's notice, especially in Ibiza."

"I never had a birthday like this!" Lexi said. "We usually play a family game of football or capture the flag in one of our fields, and then have a picnic. But with all my brothers, there is *never* enough cake!"

"Same here. My mom usually plans a small party," Sefu said. "She makes a cake, decorates it with flowers and fruit—but she'd never go for llamas or bouncy houses. I'd be happy just playing video games all day, but her cake is reeeeeally good."

"That sounds really nice," said Caleb. "Usually, my parents take me out to dinner at some fancy restaurant in whatever city we were traveling in that year. There's strange food stacked up in the shape of a tower or served on, like, a log with moss on it. And I never get a birthday cake. It's always some sort of lychee-infused foam with flecks of gold leaf sprinkled on it."

"Whoa, that sounds fancy!" said Maddie.

"Fancy, yes. But it didn't taste very good," Caleb said. "I'd rather have a party at a bowling alley or something with friends my own age."

"I think it's their way of showing you they care," Maddie said, "even if it isn't what you want." She remembered the time her parents gave her a teddy bear with a red bow around its neck for her eighth birthday, when she'd really wanted a chemistry set. But her dad had had a bear just like that one when he was a kid, and Maddie realized it was the thought, more than the gift itself, that counted. *I'd eat strange food off a log or skip birthday cake for the rest of my life it if meant I'd get to see my parents again*, she thought.

"That's deep," Chase said. "Can I use that as a lyric for a new song?"

Just then, a llama poked its head over Doug's shoulder and licked a smear of icing off his cheek.

"I guess this one likes me," said Doug as the pop star and the super spies burst into laughter.

CHAPTER 18

Chi fa per sé fa per tre.
If you want something done right, do it yourself.

As the party started winding down, Maddie went inside the mansion to change out of her wet bathing suit, followed by a llama wearing a sky-blue party hat. The sunlight was fading a bit, and Maddie wondered if they'd spend the night here. After all, they didn't have another clue to follow, and there was an empty day in the schedule before Chase's next slew of performances (He had changed his late-night show in Madrid to an "open air pop-up musical-and-shopping experience at a later date.").

If only she had that notebook, they could have examined it for schematics for the Future Predictor—and that would bring Maddie one step closer to building it herself.

But the notebook is gone, she thought with a sigh. And then she remembered something. It was only 99 percent gone. Most of a page had torn off in her hand as the notebook blew out the minivan door. *Maybe that page is still there!* Maddie thought, running toward Chase's front lawn, where the minivan had parked itself after its repairs.

She tried to find her way back to Chase's front door but got turned around in the labyrinthine mansion. It was hard to know where you were, since the entire estate was decorated with portraits of Chase.

Just on the first floor, Maddie stumbled into a video arcade, a skating rink, an entire indoor tennis court, and a bedroom that seemed to have a thoroughbred horse living in it. The horse looked up from its hay and neighed loudly at Maddie. "Sorry, big fella," she said. "Any idea how to get out of here?" The horse tilted its head to the left, which Maddie figured was as good a direction as any other.

She closed the door and headed left, finally finding the front door they had entered through. She ran out and over to the van. "Please let that page from da Vinci's notebook still be there," Maddie said to herself. She peered under her seat in the van and found the crumpled page, feeling a surge of happiness. She ran back through the mansion, to the pool, to show her friends.

"Hey, guys, look at this!" Maddie said, running over to the edge of the pool, where the others lazed around on oversized unicorn-shaped floaties. She took a few steps back—she wasn't going to risk this last page getting wet. She laid it out on the picnic table and examined it as the others climbed out of the floaties and dried off using towels with Chase's face emblazoned on them. The writing on the yellowed page was in a scrawling, more loopy handwriting than da Vinci's. And there was something else different from the other notes she'd seen in da Vinci's mirror script.

"I think someone else wrote in this," Maddie said. "Look." She pointed to the handwriting, then compared it to another of da Vinci's notebooks on her phone. "See? It's different."

Maddie tried to read the lines from the saved page aloud, but they made no sense: "Sr mbhcb xm . . ."

The agents stared at what appeared to be gibberish. Caleb leaned forward. "I think it's a code!" He bent over the page, tracing the lines with his finger. "Anyone have a pencil?"

Maddie pulled a pencil from behind her ear and handed it to Caleb, along with a piece of paper. Caleb worked, writing out long strings of letters as the others watched:

GLYD CME WCOO FKW YVVCKHW LICX QYNI.
WYY KEWR EWC ISSB FCCX KEWAVI. RRI IOC
NVELDW GDW DYSR YJ QDSLO YNYR RRI YBRM.

"It's a Vigenère cipher!" Caleb said excitedly.

"Huh?" Lexi said, looking confused.

Caleb noticed the blank looks on the other teammates' faces. "It uses a form of polyalphabetic substitution to hide its message!" He could tell he wasn't ringing any bells. "I wrote my last holiday card using a Vigenère cipher!"

"That was a holiday card?" asked Lexi. "Sorry, I couldn't crack it."

"Me neither," Maddie admitted quietly.

"Nor could I," said Sefu.

"I tried!" said Doug. "For about five minutes, and then I got a headache."

"Well, that explains why nobody wrote back," said Caleb, continuing his codebreaking. After a moment, he unfurrowed his brow. "Got it!"

"How?" asked Maddie.

"To solve a Vigenère cipher, you need a keyword. And in our case, what have we been looking for?"

"A key to the future," said Lexi.

"Exactly," said Caleb. "So I tried out the keyword"—he paused dramatically—"key."

He held up the secret message:

WHAT YOU SEEK HAS ALREADY BEEN MADE.
YOU MUST USE YOUR BEST MUSCLE. THE KEY
PLANTS ITS FOOT OF STONE UPON THE ARNO.

"Ohhhkay," Lexi said. "But what the heck does it mean?"

"We're seeking the Future Predictor!" said Chase. "But does that mean . . . ?"

"That the future-prediction device 'has already been made'? That it actually exists?" said Maddie. *It's not possible*, she thought. Da Vinci only theorized the device, he never built one. . . . *Or did he?*

Doug's eyes widened with this news. "So this thing might really be out there somewhere? Not just the designs for it?"

"Whoever wrote this page seemed to think so," said Maddie. "And if the Future Predictor is real . . . then we have to find it before anyone else does."

Doug squirmed out of his water wings and pushed his third serving of cake to the other side of the table. His passion for all things Illuminati had overtaken his interest in continuing the birthday festivities, Maddie noticed.

"But what is our best muscle?" Sefu said, pointing to the line on the page.

"I'd have to say my quads," Lexi said.

Use your best muscle seemed familiar to Maddie. It rang a bell, deep in her memory. "That's something my parents used to say. They were obsessed with these old boxing movies set in Philadelphia. The boxer was pumped up, right? But his trainer would tell him, 'The mind is your best muscle.'"

"That makes sense," Doug said. "But what about the foot? Keys don't have feet."

"Maybe it's a musical key?" Caleb said, remembering their past adventure in New York City.

"Hmmmm," Maddie said. "It feels to me more metaphorical. But what kind of key has a foot of stone?"

"Well, there are such things as footstones, which are grave markers. Maybe we're looking for someone's grave?" said Caleb.

Maddie was lost in thought. Her parents always told her that her mind was her best muscle. And now that phrase was popping up in a hidden notebook. *Can it be a coincidence?* Maddie wondered. And what was a code that translated to modern-day English doing in da Vinci's secret notebook?

Sefu began typing on his S.M.A.R.T.W.A.T.C.H.

"Are you writing code?" Lexi asked.

"I'm doing a simple search," Sefu said. "See—foot of stone—tons of results. Let me narrow this down a bit."

Sefu typed some more and then paused. "Look at this. It's a poem by Henry Wadsworth Longfellow."

"Oh!" Doug said. "He was rumored to be—"

"Illuminati," said the other super spies, all at once.

"But he wasn't around in da Vinci's time," Caleb noted. "Longfellow was born hundreds of years later."

Sefu read the poem:

Taddeo Gaddi built me. I am old,
Five centuries old. I plant my foot of stone
Upon the Arno, as St. Michael's own

Sefu repeated the line: "I plant my foot of stone upon the Arno."

"The Arno is a river in Italy," Caleb said.

"And the title of the poem is 'The Old Bridge at Florence,' published in 1875," said Sefu.

"But how could a poem from 1875 end up in this notebook?" Doug wondered.

"Maybe someone added it later," said Maddie. "After all, the handwriting is different."

"So somebody else had access to da Vinci's most secret notebook before we did," said Caleb.

"Da Vinci definitely didn't write that page," said Maddie. "The code is in English, not Italian." There was definitely something strange about this. She had a feeling someone was speaking directly to her through these pages, leading her to the future prediction device.

At least, she *hoped* they were still getting closer. After all, if the Old Bridge in Florence turned out to be another dead end, then they were officially out of clues.

CHAPTER 19

Nessuna nuova, buona nuova.

No news is good news.

"Change of plans, Shonda!" Chase said on the phone with his tour manager. "Cancel my next two performances. I'm going to Florence!" Maddie could hear a muffled, tinny voice on the other end that didn't sound too pleased.

Maddie started to clean up after the party, stuffing paper plates into a trash bag. "Hold up, fam," said Chase, shaking his head. "I have a whole staff to take care of cleanup." But leaving the cleaning to someone else just wasn't in Maddie's DNA. She'd never had anyone clean up after her—ever. So she kept at it. "Okay, okay," said Chase, "I guess we can give my cleaning crew the night off." The superstar picked up a trash bag, held it in front of his face as if he'd never seen one before, and started cleaning.

Maddie nearly shrieked a minute later when she saw Chase toss a silver tray into the trash. "Chase! That's not garbage!"

"You sure?" asked Chase. "I can always buy another one." Maddie took a deep breath and let it out.

"Just leave it," she said. "Trust me."

With all the super spies plus Chase working, the mansion and pool area were both shipshape in just a few minutes.

"I think it's time to follow our next clue to the Old Bridge," said Sefu.

"Right," said Maddie. "Are you coming with us?"

Sefu shook his head. "I'll be more help if I'm working from Camp Minerva." He stepped into his flying van. "I suggest you get a move on." Maddie nodded.

"Oh," said Sefu, "and thank you, Chase, for a wonderful day."

Chase made a heart shape with his hands and held it over his heart. "I got you, player," he said.

"We should get moving too," said Maddie. She, Lexi, Caleb, Doug, and Chase hopped into their flying van. The car lifted into the air, and the group discussed their next move.

"We've got to follow this lead and go straight to the Old Bridge," Maddie said.

"The Ponte Vecchio," Caleb corrected her. "That's what everyone in Firenze calls it."

"I thought we were going to Florence!" Lexi said.

"*Firenze* is what the Italians call Florence," said Chase. Maddie gave the singer a surprised look. "I'm an international pop star!" he explained. "It's my job to know these things."

Just then, a loud ringing sound emanated from the minivan's speakers. Volkov's face appeared on the center console's holo-screen, looking just as terrifying as she did in the flesh.

"Agents," Volkov said in her clipped, brusque tone. "What exactly are you doing?"

"Uhh, the mission?" Maddie said.

"And how is the asset?" Volkov demanded.

"What's up, ma'am?" Chase crooned. "Everything's chill."

"Chill? You expect me to believe that? Then what is . . . THIS?" Volkov's face disappeared as a scroll of images and social media posts streamed down the screen. Headlines blared *Chase Chance Takes His Chances!* and *Pop Star Leaps from Historic Building*, accompanied by photos of the super spies parachuting from Westminster Abbey.

"We can explain," Maddie said, knowing full well that she could *not* explain. Their photos were all over the internet, and Chase's famous face was clearly visible.

"This kind of stunt not only compromises the mission, it compromises the Illuminati itself. You were careless to do something like this. What were you thinking?" Volkov's voice got louder, and her Eastern European accent got heavier.

Maddie's heart sank. They were in big trouble. "You see, Commander Volkov," she said nervously, "we, uh, hit some dead ends in our investigation. . . ."

"Investigation?" asked Volkov. "Your job was to keep Chase safe."

"But we had to find out what was causing all the disasters that kept targeting him—"

"And you failed to do this?" accused Volkov.

"Well . . . ," said Maddie, "we haven't succeeded . . . yet. But we started looking for da Vinci's lost notebook and—"

"Stop right there. The very existence of such a treasure is classified," said Volkov. "For good reason."

"But now we think that the lost notebook will point us to

something that will definitely keep Chase safe: da Vinci's Future Predictor!" said Maddie. "He really built one! We think. And we can find it! We think!" She didn't mention her personal reasons for wanting to use the device.

"I didn't want to have to tell you this," Volkov said, letting out a long, serious-sounding sigh. Everyone leaned away from the holographic image, scared of what Volkov would say next. She continued, "Years ago, three of our finest agents went looking for the Future Predictor. They had credible intel and were close to securing it for the Illuminati so we could keep it from falling into evil hands." Volkov took in a dramatic breath.

"Two of those agents went rogue, and then completely disappeared. And the third—well, I believe you know him: Zander Lyon."

Everyone gasped. Zander Lyon was famous for his inventions, his adrenaline-fueled billionaire lifestyle of helicopter-ski-jumping, and his best-selling series of self-help books. He was less famous for the fact that he'd betrayed the Illuminati and become a criminal mastermind, only to be stopped from his evil plan by Maddie and her team.

"Since you have failed to protect Chase and safeguard his world tour, you have failed your mission. I'm ordering you to report back to Camp Minerva. Immediately."

"But—" Maddie started.

"It's an order," Volkov said. "I'm not losing any more good agents to this dangerous goose chase."

"Some goose chases are fun," said Lexi.

"Enough!" cried Volkov. "The search for the Future Predictor is far too risky, and there are some very bad people who would stop at nothing to get it. I will determine the appropriate consequences for all of you." Volkov abruptly hung up the video call.

The agents slumped in their seats, deflated. "I'm sorry, team," Maddie said.

"I guess that's that," Doug said softly.

"We did try," Lexi said.

"And it was an order. Obeying official orders from ranking members is the first line of the Illuminati vow we signed when we became full agents," Caleb said.

"But something doesn't add up!" Maddie said. "Every mission we do is dangerous, and we've dealt with ruthless criminals before. Why would Volkov shut *this* one down, and then quickly hang up like that? There's something she's not telling us."

"I think we should keep looking for it," Chase said. "I can't go back on tour thinking something awful is going to happen to me any second!"

Maddie tapped her phone nervously on her knee. "What if we went . . . *rogue*?" she asked. "We've done it before. Remember when Zander Lyon stole the Statue of Liberty? That was super dangerous and we ended up saving the world!"

"I don't want to make Volkov angry," said Doug. "She scares me."

Caleb brought up what happened to the other agents.

"If Zander Lyon and two other agents wanted this device so badly they went rogue for it, we could be walking into major trouble."

"Good point," said Maddie.

"Also," Lexi said, "if we go rogue *again*, it may be our last Illuminati mission . . . ever."

"Another good point," said Maddie with a sigh. When they'd last gone rogue to find the Statue of Liberty, they were taking a big gamble. She wasn't sure they'd be forgiven . . . twice.

Chase threw his hands in the air. "I can't believe what I'm hearing!" he said. "We need that machine! Y'all know I give a hundred and ten percent every night. How am I supposed to do that if I'm in danger all the time, fam?"

Maddie thought for a moment. She really wasn't ready to give up yet. "Maybe we can find out more about those agents who went rogue—and see what happened to them. Sefu, can you find anything in the Illuminati records?"

"On it!" Sefu said. "I'm not back at HQ yet, but I can access most of the Illuminati's files from my minivan . . . sort of. I'll have to hack in, but I will be able to gain remote access." The team heard him make a few keystrokes on his holo-tab. "I'm in," he said.

"What do you see?" asked Maddie.

"I'm running a search, cross-referencing with membership lists, rogue agent alerts, and mission stats, along with anything having to do with the future prediction device.

184

Oh," he said, pausing. "This is fascinating. Maddie—remember when we tried to look up more about da Vinci's lost notebooks at the library at Camp Minerva, and it was restricted?"

"Yeah," Maddie said. "We didn't have enough security clearance and set off some alarms."

"Well, because I had to hack into the system just now, I seem to have gotten past the alarms," explained Sefu. "There are pages and pages of details about da Vinci's lost notebook and the Future Predictor. But it doesn't appear as if anyone has ever found the instructions to build one."

"What about the rogue agents Volkov mentioned?" asked Maddie. "Were they successful?"

"It doesn't say," said Sefu. "Their files are almost totally erased."

"Well, who are they?" Caleb asked.

Sefu was quiet for a moment.

"Sefu?" Maddie asked. "You still there."

"S. Robinson and R. Robinson," Sefu said. "Went rogue and disappeared without a trace three years ago."

Maddie's heart stopped. S. Robinson? She knew that name. And R. Robinson? She knew that, too. She sank in her seat, shaking her head. It couldn't be true. It didn't make sense!

"Robinson," said Lexi. "Like you, Maddie!"

"Yeah. Ha, coincidence," said Maddie. Her face flushed. Not only did she know an S. and an R. Robinson, but the people she knew by those names had in fact disappeared three years ago.

S. Robinson was Sandra.

R. Robinson was Robert.

They were her parents.

CHAPTER 20

Ai mali estremi, estremi rimedi.
Desperate times call for desperate measures.

Maddie didn't mention that fact to her fellow teammates. It burned her up inside to keep the truth from her best friends, but what could she do? They would never trust her again if they found out her own parents had worked with Zander Lyon and betrayed the Illuminati.

She felt dizzy. "You feeling okay?" asked Doug. "I get motion sickness in these flying cars sometimes, too."

"Yeah, I'm just motion sick," said Maddie weakly. In fact, she was trying to reconcile these rogue agents with the kind, loving parents she remembered. And worse, all signs pointed to another horrible truth. She and her team knew a powerful inventor was after Chase. Could their mysterious foe be . . . her parents?

Are my parents the bad guys? Maddie felt sick at the thought.

A text message pinged on Maddie's phone. It was from . . . Lexi.

Not super great at girl talk but . . . do you need to talk? You don't look so good.

Another text bubble appeared on the screen.

R. and S. Robinson are your parents . . . right?

Maddie looked up from her phone at Lexi, who looked back at her with a serious, knowing expression. It was really kind of her not to blurt this out to the whole group, especially since she could tell that Maddie was shaken up. The boys continued to bicker about the best course of action, and Maddie typed back:

Yeah. I'm afraid . . .

Maddie typed and deleted about three different answers before deciding on:

I'm afraid they're not who I thought. What if they're the bad guys?

Lexi's response was almost immediate.

We'll figure it out. Together.

Gratitude for her friend swelled inside her, followed by another feeling: determination.

"Let's find that Future Predictor," said Maddie. If her parents were mixed up in all this, then it was her responsibility to find them. And if she had to—gulp—to stop them.

"What about Volkov?" Caleb asked. He didn't seem convinced. "She told us—"

"We know the risks," Maddie said. "We could be kicked out of the Illuminati forever. Or worse. If we run into trouble, we won't be able to count on our fellow agents to rescue us. We could be—"

"Hurt," said Chase.

"Killed," said Lexi.

"We could have our minds wiped," said Doug. "And we wouldn't even remember that we were friends."

Caleb and Lexi exchanged wary glances.

"But once we find the Future Predictor, Volkov will have to forgive us," said Maddie. "Right?"

She looked around. "Right?"

The other agents blinked back at her, clearly torn.

"We started this mission," Maddie continued. "And it's our job to finish it. The Illuminati tried to hide the existence of the Future Predictor. We're the only ones who know about it—which means we're the only ones who can find it. And once we find the device, we can use it to save Chase. But not just Chase! We can use it to save the world again and again!"

"I need you guys!" said Chase.

"I need you, too," said Maddie. "All of you. When we work together, there's nothing we can't do."

Doug nodded. "I'm in."

"Me too," said Caleb.

"I can't say no to you, sis!" said Lexi.

"I don't know if I get a vote," said Sefu over the minivan's speaker, "but I would vote yes."

189

"Yes!" cried Maddie. "Sefu, cloak our location and communication. We're going rogue."

Sefu sighed. "Then I am not safe advising you from Camp Minerva. I'll reroute my flying van so I can be your eye in the sky in Florence."

Maddie's minivan landed on the outskirts of Florence. The group made their way on foot through the city, admiring the gorgeous Cathedral of Santa Maria del Fiore, with its giant red dome and distinctive white walls covered in green and red designs.

The super spies walked down a street lined with restaurants and gelato shops. Maddie breathed in the tantalizing smell of fresh pasta, but she was in no mood to eat—her stomach had felt twisted since Sefu's bombshell about her parents. She tried to stuff those swirling thoughts deep down, forcing herself to focus on the task at hand. Once they'd found the device, she could use it find out the truth.

Following verbal directions from Sefu, the group hurried down various Florentine streets until they reached the Mercato Nuovo, a huge enclosed market surrounded by stone columns and a ceiling of tall, rounded arches. Maddie thought she saw someone ducking behind a column but realized it was probably just a tourist. Just because her parents were maybe-probably-almost-definitely bad guys didn't mean everyone was. They kept walking, but Maddie was on high alert.

As they passed the fountain of Neptune, they paused to admire the statue at the center of the fountain. A group of Italian teenagers approached the group. "Excuse me, aren't you Chase Chance?" a girl asked in accented English.

Chase smiled, flattered to be recognized, even in his baggy American tourist disguise. "Guilty as charged," he crooned, doing a mini moonwalk.

"*È lui!*" the girl said to her friends, and they squealed with excitement. "Selfie?" the girl asked. Chase joined the group as the girl held out her phone. "With X-tra cred-it we'll get throoooooooooouuuugh," they all sang, snapping dozens of photos.

Just as the group walked away, still singing Chase's song, a low-pitched rumble sounded. Windows rattled in nearby walls, and an alarm began to wail. A flock of pigeons pecking at the sidewalk took sudden flight in an explosion of flapping wings. Doug ducked to avoid them, even though they were two dozen feet away.

The ground began to shimmy and shake with force. Maddie saw an old man topple over and ran to help him up, nearly falling herself as the ground shifted back and forth beneath her feet. "Stay under here," she said, leading the old man under a stable archway.

"What's happening?!!" yelled Doug.

"Not again!" yelled Chase.

"I think it's an earthquake!" yelled Caleb.

Maddie heard the noise first—the crash of glass as store

windows were ripped apart by the quake—before she felt it. She was falling, as if in slow motion, as the ground convulsed.

Everyone had fallen down and was struggling to get back on their feet. Nearby passersby helped each other up and screamed as a few chunks of concrete fell off a building, just a few feet away from the super spies.

"*Stai attento!*" someone yelled, running down the street, shielding their head from falling debris with their arms.

Sefu's voice crackled over their ear-comms. "Looks like an earthquake, but it's only affecting a few-block radius. Get to safety!"

The agents ran, heading toward a doorway to shelter under, when the tall statue of Neptune started to rock on its pedestal of a stone chariot and horses.

"Watch out!" screamed Maddie as the statue wobbled. She picked up Doug and lugged him to safety. Meanwhile, Lexi leaped onto the rim of the fountain and reached up with her strong arms, bracing the legs of the statue to stabilize it.

Just as suddenly as it started, the rumbling stopped. Lexi cautiously stepped away from the statue. Maddie tried to put Doug back on the ground, but he clung to her like a koala. Chase and Caleb untangled themselves from where they had fallen.

"Is everyone okay?" Maddie asked, scanning her team for visible injuries.

"I think so," said Caleb, though his face was incredibly pale.

Chase patted himself down. He made a weird movement with his head, as if he were making sure it was still attached to his body. "All good!" he said, though he looked shaken.

"How did whoever is targeting Chase know he's in Florence?" Maddie asked. "It's not on the tour schedule!"

"Maybe someone's following us," said Caleb. "And then making 'accidents' happen when we let our guard down." Maddie thought back to the shadowy figure she'd seen hiding behind a column. And to the light she'd seen on the catwalk of Le Zenith after Chase's disco-ball explosion. And to the black-haired girl who'd stared at her during the lightning storm outside Westminster Abbey. Could there be people after them—or the device? Who else know about it, other than the team?

"We have to get to the bottom of this," said Lexi as the group of super spies hurried the rest of the way to the Ponte Vecchio. They split up into two groups, with Maddie, Caleb, and Lexi in one, and Doug and Chase in the other, walking down either side of the bridge so that they could cover more ground. Sefu zoomed overhead in the minivan, with the invisibility shield up, scanning the area from above.

Maddie, Caleb, and Lexi took the right-hand side, walking through throngs of pedestrians along the stone street, examining the buildings, sidewalk, and street itself for any sort of clue.

The street was crowded, and lined with shops selling everything from high-end jewelry to tacky souvenirs.

Maddie spoke into her ear-comm. "Sefu? Chase? Doug? Find anything yet?"

"Nothing out of the ordinary," Sefu said.

"Nada," Doug said.

"I found something!" said Chase.

"What?" asked Maddie excitedly.

"I found a really cool hat, and I think I should buy one for each of us," said Chase.

"Um, thanks, Chase, but we can shop for souvenirs *if* we find what we're really looking for," Maddie said.

They walked up and down the bridge, seeing nothing unusual—no Illuminati symbols, nothing that looked like the Future Predictor. Maddie's spirits sank. She sat down on the curb and put her head on her knees. *Maybe the Old Bridge has nothing to do with da Vinci. What if we disobeyed Volkov for nothing? And what if we all get in trouble because of me?*

"Look!" Caleb said. "It's a da Vinci–themed gift shop. Maybe it will give us some ideas."

Maddie's ears pricked up. *Worth a shot*, she figured.

The group streamed into the shop, pretending to browse, but really examining every inch of the store for clues. It was filled with shelves and tables and display cases overflowing with Leonardo da Vinci–themed ornaments, mugs, pens, postcards, plus mini replicas of the *Mona Lisa.*,

"Who's the naked, long-haired guy with four arms and legs?" asked Chase, pointing to a large poster.

"The Vitruvian Man," said Maddie. "Da Vinci's design." The anatomical drawing was plastered all over pot holders, tea towels, and other inexpensive gifts.

"*Buon giorno!*" the shopkeeper greeted them. Maddie hadn't noticed her at first, because she looked *very* much like the *Mona Lisa*, and she'd been sitting so still behind the cash register. She walked out from behind the counter and gestured to a shelf full of *Mona Lisa* figurines.

"These are very nice," she said. "I'll give you a good price if you buy five of them."

Doug stared at the woman, then at the figurines, then back at her. "Did anyone ever tell you that you look just like . . . ?"

"*Sì.*" The woman smiled.

"Is that why you have a whole store dedicated to da Vinci?" Lexi asked.

"It started with the *Mona Lisa*. Here in Italy, we call her by her real name, *La Gioconda*. It's a name that also means happiness."

"Chill," said Chase.

"Happiness right on Ponte Vecchio. Happiness on a mug. Happiness on a T-shirt. Great business idea, no?" She held up a T-shirt against Caleb's chest, frowned, then exchanged it for a shirt with a collar. "Much better. Buy this one."

"Did da Vinci ever visit the Old Bridge? I mean, uh, the Ponte Vecchio?" asked Maddie, trying out an Italian accent.

"*Sì, sì*," said the shopkeeper. "The legends say the genius da Vinci would pace this bridge over and over, until he was struck by inspiration. The legends also say he kept a workshop here, on the bridge, so that he could work while his inspiration was new. Of course, those are just legends," the woman said, with a mischievous smile.

Suddenly two shadows crossed in the front of the store. Running. Maddie's instincts went into high gear—tourists and shoppers wouldn't run like that. A figure dressed in a fedora and trench coat backtracked in front of the store, separated from Maddie by only a few inches and a frosted window. The cloaked person tapped a hidden earpiece. "I thought I spotted them," they said with a Spanish accent. The voice sounded feminine, but Maddie couldn't place it.

We are *being followed*, she realized. Her body tensed up for a fight.

"Ten-four," the figure said. "Heading to the rendezvous point now." With that, they ran off. Maddie took a breath.

"Team, we have to get out of here. Someone's after us," she said.

"Who?" Doug asked.

"I don't know, but they're close," said Maddie.

"Could they be other agents sent to bring us back to HQ?" Caleb asked.

"Or whoever is after me?" asked Chase.

Maddie gulped. "I don't want to find out."

They hurried out the back of the shop, finding themselves at the dead end of a narrow alley. Just then, two figures appeared at the end of the alley, sprinting toward the super spies.

"Uh-oh," Caleb said.

"What are we gonna do?" said Chase, searching for some way to escape. The figures were about thirty feet away.

"Run!" said Lexi. The super spies ran back into the shop, making a beeline for the front door. Chase crashed into a spinning rack of postcards, knocking it over.

"Sorry, miss!" he shouted as he picked himself up and kept running. He took a stack of bills from his pocket and tossed it to the *Mona Lisa*–look-alike shopkeeper.

"*Grazie!*" she yelled as the two people in trench coats burst into the store through the back door. The young shopkeeper bravely pushed herself in front of them, blocking their way and buying the super spies a few precious seconds to get ahead of their pursuers.

They were back on the Old Bridge. The bridge had

once been home to butchers and farmers, but now it was a busy shopping center packed with tourists. Every space was filled with street vendors selling jewelry and souvenirs. The spies had to push through the crowds. For a moment, Maddie lost sight of her team. "Where is everyone?" she said into her earpiece.

"Keep moving to the eastern side of the bridge!" said Sefu, who was hovering fifty feet above them in the invisible minivan. "I'll pick you up!"

Maddie looked behind her. She could hear tourists shouting, "Watch it!" as her pursuers pushed them out of the way and got closer and closer to her. The crowd was so dense, she could barely see two feet in front of her.

"Guys, wait for me!" said Chase into his earpiece. "I'm in the Superstar Division, remember? I've never had to run for my life before!"

"You can do it, Chase!" Doug said into his earpiece. "Just give it one hundred and ten percent!"

The super spies were only halfway across the bridge and Maddie could feel that whoever was chasing them was now just a few feet away. She turned back, catching only glimpses of their fedoras zigging and zagging through the crowd, getting closer and closer to Maddie's position.

"Don't let them get me!" cried Chase. "I still want to put out a country album to expand my fan base!"

"Who would want to hurt Chase?" asked Doug.

"I thought you all were supposed to be experts at this

stuff!" said Chase. "But they're gaining on us!"

Chase was right. "Who are these guys?" asked Maddie into her earpiece. *They're clearly highly trained. But by who?*

"I've got eyes on your pursuers," Sefu said from the flying van. "And by the looks of it, they're Illuminati!"

CHAPTER 21

Quando si chiude una porta, si apre un portone.
When one door closes, a bigger door opens.

Maddie whipped around and pulled off the fedora of one of the agents who was chasing them. It was a girl about Maddie's age. She had long, straight black hair and sharp black eyebrows. It took a moment, but Maddie recognized her. It was the girl from the lightning storm! She had to admit she was a bit relieved it wasn't her parents. If they really were bad guys, she wasn't ready to face them yet.

The other agent's hat blew off in the wind, and Maddie recognized the blond pompadour instantly.

Ugh, *Killian*, she thought. He was as highly trained as the rest of them, and he had a grudge against Maddie. She knew he'd be thrilled to be the one to bring her down, so that she could be reprimanded—or punished—for going rogue.

"Aha! I knew I'd find you!" said Killian, practically licking his lips with delight. "The ragtag team of not-so-super spies."

Maddie pulled out her hyper-phone and pushed a button to activate "skunk mode." She pointed it directly at them, and a stream of stinky spray hit both Killian and his partner right in the face.

"Ugh!" Killian screamed as he tried to wipe it off and it got all over his hands.

Sefu's panicked voice blared in their earpieces. "I can't get to you before Killian does—you need to get out of there!"

Maddie and her crew ran, desperately trying to get to the side of the bridge for a ride from Sefu.

"I know what you're doing, Maddie!" Killian shouted after them. "You won't get to your friend's van. And even if you did . . ." Maddie looked back over her shoulder as Killian made a few swipes on his S.M.A.R.T.W.A.T.C.H.

"What the—" Sefu cried into his earpiece. "Killian's taken control of the van! I'm floating but I can't move!"

"You're on official Illuminati frequencies, you fools," said Killian. "I've been listening to you since you were assigned to guard Chase."

Maddie stopped in her tracks. Where could she go? She'd left her team with nowhere to run. *Splitting up is our best chance*, she thought. *If Killian wants to take me in, maybe I can give myself up and give the rest of the team a chance to escape.*

"Everyone, I think I saw something! An escape!" said Lexi. With her blue hair, it was easy to spot Lexi among the crowd. She squeezed into the tight space between two buildings into a back alley.

"Get to Lexi's location!" said Maddie. "Evasive maneuvers!" She ducked and darted to confuse their attackers as she made her way to Lexi. The rest of the team followed.

"We lost Killian," said Maddie. "For a moment."

Lexi pointed to what she had seen. A plain wooden door—but in the exact center was a golden triangular coin dulled by time. On it was carved a symbol familiar to Maddie and her team: the golden triangle of the Illuminati.

"Well, that's interesting," Caleb said. The group ran over to the door. Chase stepped aside and swooped his arm toward the door in a grand gesture, looking at Lexi. "I believe this is your specialty."

Lexi smiled. She gave the centuries-old door a kick, hard enough to break it. "Oops," she said.

The golden triangle coin popped off the door and lay at Maddie's feet. *This is a souvenir worth saving*, she thought as she picked it up.

She took a step inside. Her team followed her. It was pitch dark, and the floor was slanted.

"What now?" said Doug. "This is a little stressful."

Maddie took a step backward, feeling for the wall in front of her. She just needed a second to think. But there *was* no wall. She tumbled forward. "Aaaaahhh!!!!" she yelled as everything went dark.

Maddie woke up a half second later on a pile of garbage bags. She was in some sort of basement room, where trash waited to be taken out. At least all the garbage bags were tied tightly. She looked up to the opening she'd just unceremoniously fallen from.

"Aaaahhh!!!"

Lexi plopped out, right on top of Maddie. "Move it, sister! Everyone else is behind me!" The two of them quickly climbed off the garbage bags as Doug, Caleb, and finally Chase tumbled out of the chute, landing on top of each other with three loud thuds.

The super spies got up and brushed themselves off.

"I can't believe there was a time when I wanted to be a full-on agent, like you all," said Chase. "I didn't realize there'd be so much falling and garbage involved."

"Everyone okay?" asked Lexi.

"How's my hair?" asked Chase. The singer's famous swoop had flattened in the front and gone wavy in the back. It looked exactly like the haircut of someone who had fallen down a dusty chute and landed in garbage. "Still looks . . . dreamy," said Lexi.

"No," said Maddie. "It looks crazy."

"Not a good look," said Caleb. "Don't lie to the man, Lexi."

"Here, let me fix it." Doug formed Chase's hair back to its trademark shape. "Good as new."

Lexi blushed. "I was just trying to say his hair always looks nice!"

"Thanks, fam," said Chase.

"Let's move, guys," said Maddie. They followed an open doorway out of the basement room, and the team found themselves in a musty, dark passageway, lit by flickering candles.

"We must be underground," Caleb said. "Sefu, can you hear us? And can you see where we are?"

"I've got ears on you," Sefu said. "I'm using a mix of radar, X-rays, and LIDAR technology to see where you guys are. And I scrambled the signal so it can't be tracked. It looks like a passage that leads under the city. Walk east. There should be a doorway or an opening."

The group huddled together, gripping onto each other, walking slowly and cautiously through the dark passage. After several twists and turns, a pattern of light appeared from a metal grate in the ceiling.

"Where are we, Sefu?" Maddie whispered.

"You appear to be directly underneath the Palazzo Vecchio," Sefu said.

Maddie, Caleb, Chase, and Doug lifted Lexi up, and she slid the heavy grate from the opening. She pulled herself up, then reached down to help the others climb up through the opening.

"Hurry if you can," said Sefu. "Killian and his friend are close behind."

They heard two distant thuds and the pounding of approaching footsteps.

The super spies emerged from the grate into an indoor courtyard lined with wide, ornately carved columns supporting rounded archways carved with even more designs. The walls and ceiling were covered with faded but beautiful paintings in soft reds, greens, and blues, with a central fountain shaped like a child and a dolphin on an octagonal base.

They ducked inside the palazzo and entered a cavernous room decorated with enormous paintings outlined in gold on every surface, including the ceiling. A huge battle scene dominated the room. The colorful image was filled with soldiers and horses, fighting with swords, falling, and dying, with a bit of green countryside visible in the top right corner.

"Well, this painting certainly isn't a da Vinci. Even I can tell that, and I'm no art connoisseur," Lexi said, mispronouncing it as "coin-o-saur."

"You're right," Caleb said. "It's not da Vinci, it's Giorgio Vasari. And it's not a painting, it's a fresco, which means painted on plaster. Not canvas or wood. Directly on the wall."

"Fresco, Frisco, Fresca—I don't care what it is! We don't have time to waste!" Chase said. "We need to get away from that Killian guy!"

"Oh, we never have time to enjoy the art," Caleb said, sounding disappointed.

"But why would the clues lead us here? We're looking for da Vinci, not Vasari," Lexi said.

"Good question," Maddie murmured, glancing around the room. Any second, Killian and his new partner would crawl out of that grate. "Leonardo's clues led us here, so that's got to be something! Everyone, look as hard as you can. Maybe there's a symbol or something hidden in one of these paintings—I mean, frescoes."

"Well, well, well. Look at the little culture-vultures," a condescending voice echoed across the stone floor. "If you could just surrender now, that would be great."

Killian crossed his arms smugly.

"To you?" said Maddie. "Never."

Maddie caught a glimpse of Killian's custom belt buckle—the gleaming *K*—and had a revelation. "It was you on the catwalk of Le Zenith after Chase's disco ball exploded!" She looked over to Killian's partner. "And she was there during the freak lightning storm."

The girl sneered at Maddie.

"You two are the ones causing all the accidents around

Chase!" Maddie said.

"You said it yourself, Killian," said Caleb. "You've been listening to us the whole time. That's the only way someone could've known where Chase would be."

"As always, Maddie, you're oh so wrong. Why would I attack a fellow Illuminati member like Chase?" asked Killian. "I was only watching you because I knew you'd screw things up, like you always do. And when that happened, I'd be there to expose you to Volkov for the sorry screwups you all are."

"I'll show you who's a screwup—" Lexi said, raising her fists.

"But then," Killian continued, not even dignifying Lexi with a glance, "you did something even I never expected. You all went rogue. Again! And kidnapped Chase! I must say, I never really took you for the villain type, Maddie, but you're proving me wrong."

"We didn't kidnap Chase!" said Maddie. "He wanted to come with us!"

"It's true!" said Chase.

"Ah," said Killian. "A classic case of Stockholm syndrome—he's started to believe his kidnappers' lies. Never mind, I'll hand you all over to Volkov and you'll finally be kicked out of the Illuminati once and for all."

"Just leave us alone, Killian! We're looking for something important!" Maddie said. "And no matter what you think, we're *not* the villains here. You are."

Killian let out a sour-sounding laugh. "You'll never do anything important, Maddie. You're just a bunch of insignificant losers, and I'm going to send you back to your sorry lives where you belong," he said, cracking his knuckles. "Let me introduce you to my new friend, Agent Grace Garza."

The raven-haired girl with a tan complexion stepped forward and curtsied. "A pleasure," she said with a Spanish accent.

"Grace was a star ballerina when she was recruited by the Illuminati," said Killian. "But while at Camp Minerva, it seems she picked up quite a talent for the martial arts. How about a demonstration? Grace, grab the little one first."

Lexi stepped protectively in front of Doug. Caleb and Maddie exchanged glances—what were they going to do? Maddie slipped her hand into her pocket, wrapping her fingers around her hyper-phone.

Grace lunged at Lexi and Doug, who jumped backward, just out of her reach. As she chased them around the chamber, Killian looked over at Chase, Caleb, and Maddie and pulled out a piece of rope he had tucked in his belt. He twirled a rope lasso over his head.

"Lasso class," said Killian. "So American, right? Who would've thought it would ever come in handy?"

"You're outnumbered," Caleb said.

"And you're outsmarted," Killian said, and flung the

lasso toward Caleb.

But Maddie had pulled out her hyper-phone. She quickly turned her ultra-powerful flash up to its highest setting and aimed it at Killian. The blast of pure white light made Killian stumble over his own feet. "I'm blind!" he yelled.

"It's only temporary," said Maddie.

"Apprehend her, Grace!" Killian shouted as he fell to the ground.

Maddie whirled around, pressing the flash button again and aiming for Grace, who was leaping toward Maddie, leg outstretched in a flying kick. As the flash went off, Maddie sidestepped her foe's attack. Grace fell out of the air, grabbing her eyes.

"Sorry!" said Maddie. "I hope we can still be friends after this!"

Grace and Killian were both too dazed to stand. Lexi produced a length of nano-rope and, with Caleb's and Chase's help, tied their defeated attackers to a stone column.

"The karate masters I've trained with say to always respect your opponent," said Lexi. "But I'm making an exception for you." Lexi leaned down in Killian's face. "Dude, we kicked your butt!" she said. "Na na na na na!"

Killian grunted and fought against his confinement, but the nano-cord only got tighter as he struggled.

"The problem with 'insignificant losers,' Killian,"

Maddie said, "is that you always underestimate them."

"You'll pay for this, Maddie," said Killian, his voice echoing through the stone chamber. "You're going to paaaaaaaay. . . ."

CHAPTER 22

Essere in alto mare.
To be on the high seas.

"Now what?" Doug asked, his bottom lip quivering. He looked really shaken up.

Maddie stepped into the next room. Other than the limestone on the floor and walls, it was empty.

"Look, I have to admit I used to be jealous of you guys!" Chase said, his voice cracking. "Real Illuminati members get to have all sorts of cool adventures. But I don't want adventures anymore! I just want to stay safe and entertain people!"

"Maddie," Caleb said, "any idea what our next step is?"

Maddie rubbed her face in frustration. "I don't know what our next step is! We've followed the clues here, and . . ." She noticed that Caleb was systematically scanning the ceiling, the walls, and even the floor, as if looking for something.

Doug was tapping on every inch of the wall, looking for a hidden mechanism.

Chase had his eyes closed, singing softly to himself to keep calm.

Maddie looked over at Lexi, who averted her eyes. "Sorry, Maddie," said Lexi. "I'm not so good at this part."

"You're great!" reassured Maddie. "I'm glad to have you on the team." Lexi smiled. But Maddie still didn't know how to move forward.

"It's no use," she said, "We don't even know what we're looking for, and it's not like the next clue is right under our feet—"

"Ahem," said Caleb as he pointed to the floor, right at Maddie's feet.

"Huh?" Maddie crouched down. A small triangular hole was carved in between the stone panels of the floor. She reached into her pocket and pulled out the triangular coin that had been inlaid in the door Lexi kicked in. Maddie placed it carefully in the hole, and as it slid into place, a squeaking and groaning sound emanated from beneath their feet. A section of floor rotated away, revealing a spiraling stone staircase leading into darkness.

"Whoa," Doug whispered.

"After you," Maddie said, gesturing politely at the

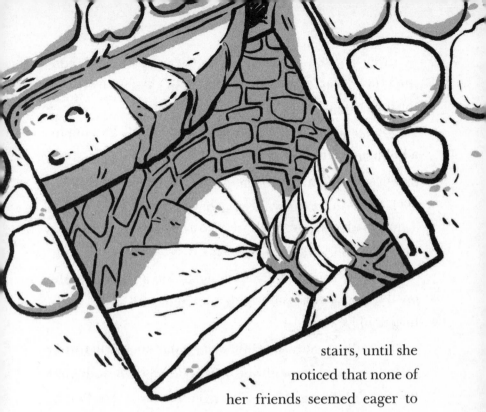

stairs, until she noticed that none of her friends seemed eager to test the stability of the six-hundred-year-old hidden stairway. "Okay, after me," she said, taking a deep breath.

As she descended, the light grew dimmer and dimmer. The stone steps were worn and crumbling. Maddie nearly slipped twice. But she made it to the bottom. "It's okay!" she yelled to her friends. "Just be careful on the way down."

When they all reached the bottom of the stairs, the stone panel slid back into place, trapping them in darkness under the floor of the Palazzo Vecchio. They all grabbed each other's hands, and Maddie lit the flashlight on her phone, illuminating a perfectly round stone room, with a doorway on either side.

A whirring sound filled the chamber, and a spindly contraption on the floor began spinning in a circle.

"What's happening?" Doug whispered.

"I'm not sure," Maddie replied.

Suddenly, a beam of light pierced the darkness, and the pale blue holographic image of a person appeared. It was an old-looking man with long hair, a long beard, and a rather pouffy hat.

Maddie knew that face. It was like seeing an old friend. "Leonardo!" she cried. Even though it was a hologram, she felt a wave of excitement at seeing her hero in the flesh. Well, sort of.

She walked up to the hologram, and it smiled at her. Maddie's jaw dropped. She had to remind herself that she wasn't looking at a real person. *But he sure looks real*, she thought. *And I have a million questions I want to ask him!*

Maddie waved. The holographic Leonardo waved back.

Maddie did a little dance and Leonardo danced back.

Maddie gave Leonardo the Illuminati's triangle salute, and the hologram saluted her right back. Maddie's team gasped in unison.

Maddie ran around Leonardo and looked all over the room, trying to find how the realistic hologram was being projected, but the tech was advanced, even for her. She wondered just how much of the real Leonardo's knowledge he held.

"I feel like I'm meeting a rock star!" she said.

"You weren't this excited when you met an *actual* rock star," sniffed Chase.

"Leonardo, you were even more of a genius than people gave you credit for," Maddie said to the hologram.

The faux Leonardo smiled. "Welcome, traveler. I know what you seek," the hologram said.

"The Future Predictor?" Maddie asked.

The hologram nodded.

"Well, how do we find it? Is it here?" she looked around excitedly.

"Motion is the root of all life," Leonardo said. "If you dare move through this space, be warned. Because it is also the root of all death." The hologram extended his arm toward to the doorway on its left, and then flickered and disappeared.

The agents stared openmouthed at the empty space where it had been.

"That was amazing!" Maddie said.

"That was disconcerting," Caleb said.

"How did he do that?" Maddie said. "We just have to go through that doorway."

"Um, I think I heard him say 'death,'" Doug whispered. "Maybe we should turn back."

"C'mon, Doug," Chase urged. "Don't you want to help me find this thing? I want my life back!"

"We'll protect you," said Lexi, flexing her biceps.

Doug looked at the doorway dubiously and at his friends. "Okay."

Maddie walked through the doorway, which led to a set of spiral stairs. They walked down, down, down several flights. The sound of rushing water echoed through the stone stairwell. It opened onto a stone ledge by an underground canal of greenish water, flowing briskly away into the darkness. An ornate wooden boat bobbed in the current, tied to a stone loop carved into the ledge.

"Is this da Vinci's boat?" asked Lexi.

"I think so," said Maddie. "He designed a ship, and this matches his drawing almost exactly."

"It's just been sitting here for hundreds of years," said Caleb. "Cool."

"It still floats," said Chase. "But do you think it's still seaworthy?"

"Only one way to find out," said Maddie. "And it's not like we have any other options."

Well, technically, they could heed Leonardo's warning and go back to Volkov to beg her forgiveness. But Maddie knew they were *so* close to finding the Future Predictor. She just knew all her problems would be solved once they found it. She couldn't turn back now. They were *all in*.

The spies and Chase piled into the boat, which was sturdy and roomy enough for all of them. Lexi untied the rope, and the boat glided into the canal. They were in some sort of underground tunnel, with dripping stone walls. The only light came from the team's flashlights, which they aimed at the darkness ahead of them. The boat rounded a curve and suddenly picked up speed. It rocked gently side to side as it whooshed through the blackness, as if they were in some sort of turbocharged waterslide. It seemed this boat was more like their flying minivan than a regular boat!

Maddie put her phone away and gripped the wooden sides of the boat. She needed to hang on! She felt a small body wedge itself next to her.

"I'm scared," Doug whispered, grabbing Maddie's arm.

"Me too," said Maddie. "But let's pretend we're excited, rather than scared. After all, we're on an adventure! Before you joined the Illuminati, did you ever think you'd be riding on an underground boat built by Leonardo da Vinci?"

"No," said Doug. "And my mom always said I had a *very* active imagination." Maddie wrapped her arm around him, squeezing him reassuringly, just like her mom used to do when she woke up after a bad dream. How could someone who hugged her at night so sweetly have been working with someone evil like Zander Lyon? Maddie didn't think her mom had the capacity to be evil, but she also never thought her mom and dad were secret Illuminati agents, either.

"Anyone know where we're going?" yelled Chase.

"No idea!" yelled Caleb. "I'll see if Sefu can track us!" But when he called Sefu, there was nothing but static. He tapped his earpiece and tried again. Nothing. "We must be too far underground." They were cut off from contact.

As the boat speeded up even more, Maddie wished she could take it apart and see what made it work. How was it getting so much power?

"Look!" Lexi cried, pointing ahead. "A light at the end of the tunnel!"

A bright semicircle of light almost blinded the super spies as all five of them tried to see what was on the other side of the opening. The boat picked up even more speed and the agents screamed as the water roared and splashed like white-water rapids. The boat shot out of the mouth of the tunnel and into dazzling sunshine. A sail suddenly unfurled from the mast, catching the wind. The boat bobbed along a huge river, lined with trees and gorgeous buildings covered in turrets, like fairy-tale castles.

"Judging by the architectural style of these castles," said Caleb, "I'd say we're somewhere in France."

"Ooh, I've always wanted to go to France," said Doug.

"We were just in Paris!" said Caleb. "Remember? You were almost killed by an exploding disco ball?"

"Oh yeah," said Doug. "I wanted to forget that . . . I guess I did!"

"This is prettier than Paris," said Lexi. "More of a country vibe."

Just then, Sefu's voice beamed into all of their earpieces. "Hello? Hello? Are you guys okay? Can you hear me?"

"Sefu!" Maddie cried, so relieved to hear his voice. "Can you track us? We're on a river. Somewhere in France, maybe?"

"I've got a lock on your location. You're on the Loire River, headed north. The next town is called Amboise. See if you can get off there. We can rendezvous in about an hour."

"Perfect," said Caleb, "if we can figure out how to stop this thing."

Farms lined the riverside. "Are those grape trees?" asked Maddie.

"Grapes grow on vines," said Lexi. "But, yup, those are grapevines!"

"This valley is where some of the world's most famous wines come from," Caleb said.

A town suddenly appeared on the left bank ahead, and the agents looked around their ship for some sort of steering device to bring the boat to shore. There was no wheel or rudder that they could find.

"Anyone see any oars?" Maddie asked.

"I say we swim for it!" said Lexi, ready to dive out of the speeding boat.

Just then the mast rotated by itself, and the wind propelled them right to a wooden dock.

"Whoa," Maddie said in awe. "Da Vinci must have invented this self-sailing boat!"

"I have a self-sailing yacht," said Chase. "But Leo did it old-school-style. Respect!"

As they bumped up against the dock, Lexi jumped off and tied the boat with the rope. She helped the others step onto the dock, and they made their way into a picturesque town of pale buildings with steep slate roofs, dwarfed by an impressive château with a large, crenellated tower.

"Now that is fancy," Lexi said. "Caleb, do you know what that big castle thing is?"

Caleb looked flattered to be asked. He cleared his throat. "That's the Château d'Amboise, if I'm not mistaken. Royalty lived there. But the really interesting fact about this town is that da Vinci lived here for the last four years of his life! In fact, I believe he's even buried here."

"Correct," Sefu said. "The king of France built a chapel on the palace grounds, where da Vinci's remains lie to this day."

Chase shivered. "Skeletons freak me out."

"Do you think that could be where the next clue is hiding?" Lexi asked.

"Um, I am *not* breaking into someone's tomb," Chase said. "So un-chill."

Caleb picked up a tourist brochure from outside a small shop. "Hey, guys! Look at this," he said. "Château du Clos Lucé—this was da Vinci's home!"

"Let's start there!" Maddie said. "We can always break into his tomb later if we don't find any other leads," she said, winking at Doug. Doug smiled. They had found a secret lab inside Ben Franklin's tomb last year.

The five of them hurried through the town to Clos Lucé, a stately pink-brick building with windows outlined in light gray stone, tucked among immaculate gardens on a lush green lawn.

"Let's explore the grounds and see what we can find," Maddie said. She had a good feeling about this place. It *felt* like a place where secrets were kept.

They entered the château and grabbed some informational pamphlets. There were other tourists milling around, getting ready to go on a tour.

"This place is, like, old," said Chase.

Maddie skimmed the pamphlet. "Apparently, King Francis I gave this château to da Vinci."

"He just gave it to him?" asked Lexi.

"Da Vinci was famous while he was alive," said Caleb. "So the king gave the house to da Vinci to convince him to move here."

Chase nodded. "I own a house in Guatemala for the same reason," he said.

The team walked through da Vinci's personal chamber. Maddie imagined the genius thinking up new ideas as he woke from the heavy wooden bed. "Can you believe it?" she said. "Da Vinci actually lived and slept and *invented* in this very room!"

In another section, the museum had reproduced many of Leonardo's inventions. "Is that . . . a helicopter?" asked Lexi.

"Yep," said Maddie, still amazed by how ahead of his

time da Vinci truly was. "He called it the Aerial Screw." Its spiral shape reminded Maddie of a swirl of soft-serve ice cream. She was amazed to see these contraptions in three dimensions, after being so familiar with the sketches in Leonardo's notebooks. "I sure would like to have a king give me a house and pay for me to invent all day," Maddie said to herself.

In da Vinci's basement workshop, a guide gave a brief tour. "Who wants to know a secret?" she asked.

"Ooh, me!" said Doug, drawing too much attention to the super spies.

"I like that enthusiasm," said the guide. "Here's something that in their day was known only to King Frances and da Vinci himself: there exists a secret underground passageway connecting this château to the Château d'Amboise, the king's home here." The guide continued, "The king and da Vinci were very close, and this allowed them to visit each other and trade ideas without unwanted ears listening in on them."

The super spies stared at each other, eyes wide. They lingered as the guide led a crowd of museumgoers into another room.

"Did you hear that?" Maddie said. "A secret passageway!"

"Sounds like a really good place to hide a clue," said Lexi, grinning.

"Indubitably," Caleb said. "Let's find it."

They split up, examining different parts of the room,

moving quickly before another tour group appeared. Maddie examined a heavy wooden cabinet, which was filled with seashells, fossils, and other objects of curiosity.

The guide called after them. "Kids? Come along to the next room," she said.

"One second!" said Maddie. "We're just very, um, enthused." The guide nodded. "Let's hurry," Maddie said to her team.

Inside the cabinet, Maddie spotted a human skull and a skeleton of a bat.

"Yikes!" said Lexi, noticing the bat.

"Leonardo studied bats to help his work with flying machines," said Maddie.

"They may have been helpful," said Lexi, "but they're still scary."

"Kids!" said the museum guide. "Please keep up with the tour!"

"Of course!" said Maddie. "Just one more second!"

Quickly, Maddie opened the cabinet and reached for the bat skeleton.

"That was added by the museum, right?" asked Lexi. "There's no way that's the original skeleton that da Vinci actually used?"

Maddie wasn't sure. But when she very carefully lifted the skeleton, the cabinet swung outward a few inches, nearly bonking her on the nose.

"You guys!" she hissed. "Look!"

The others rushed over and Lexi pulled out the cabinet away from the wall, revealing an opening in the brick
behind it.

"The secret passage!" exclaimed Caleb.

"Kids? Kids?" said the guide as she began walking back toward the room they were still in. "Come along now."

"Go, go, go!" said Maddie, hustling her friends inside the newly revealed passage.

"This is so lit!" Chase said. They filed inside, and the heavy cabinet swung shut behind them. The super spies clicked on their flashlights and followed the passageway until it branched off in several directions.

"Which way?" Caleb said, pointing his flashlight down the different passages.

"I need to think," Maddie said, sitting on the cold stone floor. She dragged her fingers through the dust on the floor as she racked her brain for any idea of what to do. "Any thoughts?"

The rest of the group shrugged. Maddie leaned back against the wall. Her head bumped against something sticking out of the wall behind her head. She turned and saw the edge of something metallic poking out from between two bricks. She pulled it loose and stared down at the circular metal object in her palm.

"It's a compass," she said. "But what are we supposed to do with it? We have GPS on our devices, anyway." She flipped it over in her hand. Maybe there'd be a secret compartment or false back or something. In the dull metal, something was inscribed in Leonardo's familiar mirror writing. Maddie quickly traced the reverse of each letter in the dust at her feet.

Ciao, Maddie, it read in elegant script.

A caval donato non si guarda in bocca.

Don't look a gift horse in the mouth.

Maddie stopped breathing for a moment. Then her heart began to race. Then she gulped.

"Does that say . . . *Maddie*?" she whispered. She held out the compass for her friends to see.

"Yep," Lexi said.

"As in . . . you?" said Caleb.

Maddie stood up and ran her fingers over the inscription. *Ciao, Maddie.* Leonardo must have inscribed this for her.

Which meant that Leonardo knew she'd find it.

Which also meant that he'd *used* the Future Predictor.

Maddie suddenly felt light-headed. Leonardo knew

about her, specifically! He'd known she'd come here, and he planned for her to find this. He must have left this message for her at least five hundred years ago! She reminded herself to breathe again. This rogue investigation was feeling a lot less like a mission and more like . . . destiny. She rotated the compass in her hand. The needle wobbled a bit but kept pointing in the same direction.

"But what does it mean?" Maddie said, in a slightly shaking voice.

"Well, it's a compass," Lexi said.

"I know that," Maddie said. "But what do we do with it?"

"A compass tells you where to go," Doug said. "It's not like you need arcane Illuminati knowledge to know that."

"Usually a compass uses the earth's electromagnetic pull to lead you north. But something tells me da Vinci built this one a little differently," said Caleb.

"We've followed da Vinci this far," Maddie said. "He hasn't led us astray yet."

She stepped to the spot where the various passages branched off. The compass pointed directly toward the opening slightly to their left. They followed it and reached the end of the passageway. Their flashlights illuminated a large wooden chest.

"It's just like a video game," said Doug. "Sefu, you'd love this."

"Let's open it!" Chase said, full of excitement. "Maybe the device is in there!"

Lexi pried open the lid and lifted out several panels of a rigid, light brown linen in thin wood and metal frames and laid them on the floor. The linen was stiffened with some sort of wax, and the frames were sturdy but light.

Caleb lifted a section and examined it. "I think some of the pieces connect together," he said, running his hands down one edge. The shape of the panel reminded Maddie of something. A drawing she had seen somewhere. She dug through the pile, pulling out various pieces of framework. She could see that someone had left her enough material to make several sets.

"I know what this is!" she cried, holding up a larger, curved section. "It's one of Leonardo's designs!" She worked quickly, asking the others to hold a panel here, hand her a section there, as she snapped and tightened the wooden and metal rods together. The overall effect was very similar to a bird's wingspan, or the bat skeleton wings in da Vinci's workshop, but with fabric in each segment.

"May I present to you," she said, "wings—for *humans!* Leonardo studied flight in animals—but he also studied human anatomy, trying to figure out how to let people fly, and here's the end result!" She quickly put together the other sets of wings—five sets in all.

"So, what are we supposed to do with these?" Lexi said, trying one wing on. "There's not enough room in here for us to try these out."

Maddie looked down at the compass. "I think we're

supposed to keep following this," she said, staring at the wall that closed off the north end of the passage.

"Let me bust through that wall!" Lexi said.

"Let's retrace our steps through the passage," suggested Caleb.

"Wait," Chase said. "Feel that?" He held out his hand near the wooden chest. The others did the same, and felt a slight breeze.

"This is an external wall," Caleb said. "We might be able to get out this way."

Lexi gave the wooden chest a hefty shove. It didn't budge. She shook out her arms. "A little help?"

The five of them gathered on one side of the chest and pushed with all their might. Slowly, the chest scraped against the floor, revealing a doorway, painted to look like the same bricks that covered the walls. They pushed open the door and found themselves on a windy ledge only a few feet wide on the back of one of the château's turrets. They were a few hundred feet from the ground—the château was tall, and built onto a hillside, which sloped sharply toward the river. The agents pressed themselves against the wall behind them, clutching their wings tightly.

"I think there's only one thing we can do," Maddie yelled. "Put on your wings! We're going to fly north!"

The super spies helped each other slide their arms into the wings and secure them with the attached leather straps.

"Ready?" Maddie yelled over the howling wind. "On

three! One . . . two . . . three!" All five of them stepped off the ledge, into nothing but air. "Everyone—FLAP!" Maddie shrieked as she started to sail downward. The buildings and concrete below did not look very soft.

The agents struggled to flap their arms, attached to the unwieldy wings, as they sank lower.

Doug screamed. Caleb closed his eyes. Maddie gulped—maybe she'd made a huge mistake.

Just then, a huge gust of wind, funneled upward by the sloped banks of the Loire, rushed up the side of the château, filling everyone's wings and lifting them high above the river.

"Wheee!" Lexi yelled. Maddie looked around and checked her team, now soaring over the river. Doug was still screaming, Caleb's eyes were closed, and Chase seemed, well, chill.

We're flying! Maddie thought, exhilarated.

"Doug! Caleb! It's okay! We're safe!" she called. She gave her wings an experimental flap, and suddenly swooped several yards up and away from the others.

"WhheeeeEEEEEooooOOOOO!" Lexi yelled as she executed a perfect loop-de-loop, three hundred feet in the air.

"Please don't let there be any pigeons this high up," Doug whimpered.

"I got you, buddy!" Lexi called. "I'll fly next to you and scare any birds away."

"Other birds are fine!" Doug said. "It's only pigeons that scare me."

They flew and flew, barely having to flap, as the wind carried them along for miles, over the green and yellow fields of the French countryside.

"We must be riding a jet stream," Caleb said. "This is, as Chase would say, totally lit."

Chase let out a loud whoop. "I've gotta sell my hang glider," he shouted. "This is way better! I feel like I'm on a trampoline!"

Maddie smiled. Even after flying in a private jet, the flying minivan, and the helicopter she'd once built out of submarine parts and chewing gum, there was nothing like this. It was amazingly peaceful and quiet. She felt connected to the air in a way she never had before, and the wings started to feel like they were really an extension of her body. *This must be what it feels like to be a bird*, she thought. She sighed in happiness, marveling at how well Leonardo had engineered this experience.

The wind carried them on, over a huge body of water.

"This is the North Sea," yelled Caleb. "See that land far off to the right? That should be Norway!"

"How far is this taking us?" said Lexi. "Not that my arms are tired."

They flew over Scandinavia (according to Caleb) and continued north. Maddie checked the compass, held tight in her outstretched hand. It still pointed north. Her face had begun to burn from the constant wind, and she started to shiver. She was grateful that they were wearing Illuminati-issued thermo-regulating hoodies, which provided some warmth. The compass continued to point north, and so they flew on.

Soon enormous ice floes appeared beneath them. A group of plump gray seals lounged on an icy cliff edge, with a vast white expanse stretching beyond.

Below, a pod of white whales breached the freezing waters. Maddie watched as water shot out of their blowholes. "That's a beluga!" she shouted to her teammates.

They flew farther and farther over snow and ice, passing a family of polar bears.

"I think we're at the North Pole!" Caleb shouted. "Maddie, check the compass!"

Maddie looked at it through the crust of frost that had built up over the flight. The compass arrow was spinning.

Suddenly, a tower of snow and ice loomed up in front of the agents. Because of the bright light bouncing off the snow, they hadn't seen it until now.

"Yikes!" Doug screamed.

"Double yikes!" Chase yelled.

"Try to stop!" Maddie yelled as they hurtled forward.

"Why didn't da Vinci invent brakes?" shouted Caleb.

We're flying too fast, Maddie realized as she headed straight for the jagged, icy mass. *We're going to smack right into it!*

Just as the flying super spies were about to crash into the
icy mountainside, a wall opened up, like an automatic door
at a grocery store, and the agents flew through the central
opening, tumbling to a halt on a bouncy, shock-absorbent
floor.

"Da Vinci's wing-suits worked!" shouted Maddie. *What
if something I invent is still useful five hundred years from now?*
she wondered.

The super spies quickly unstrapped themselves from
their wings, helping each other free their arms from the
framework. They shook out their arms and rubbed them,
bringing back circulation, as Maddie looked around.

They'd flown directly into someone's secret lair!

CHAPTER 24

Finché c'è vita c'è speranza.
While there's life, there's hope.

It was a round room with translucent walls that revealed a cloudy glimpse of the world outside the structure. When the huge doors shut, it felt like a giant snow globe, with rounded passage-ways radiating out from the outer wall. It reminded Maddie a little bit of the Franklin Institute Planetarium in Philadelphia, which she'd visited many times. At the center of the room was a wooden table holding a small contraption that looked like an old-fashioned telescope: a cone on top, with a square box underneath, and a scroll of parchment at its base.

At the base of the cone, a series of metal spirals twisted delicately from the pointy end, disappearing into a drumlike metal base with several horizontal rows. Some were etched with letters, others with numbers and roman numerals, symbols and arrows, even something that looked like Braille.

"What *is* this place?" Lexi asked.

"I hate to use a cliché phrase like 'supervillain's secret Arctic lair,'" Caleb said. "But this is absolutely a supervillain's secret Arctic lair."

Chase looked around, scanning every inch of the lair, and Doug rubbed his eyes, as if he couldn't believe what he was seeing.

Maddie continued to stare at the unusual contraption. Something about its elegant, geometric lines, the grain of the wood, and the proportions of the spirals felt so familiar. She'd never seen this sketched in a notebook, but it had the unmistakable design hallmarks of her hero, Leonardo da Vinci. Her pulse raced, and she found it hard to draw a breath. Could this really be it? The Future Predictor? Maddie circled the machine, trying to understand how it worked.

"You guys," she said. "I think this is the—"

Maddie was interrupted by the sound of pounding boots echoing off the glassy walls.

"STAY RIGHT WHERE YOU ARE!" a male voice boomed.

Maddie froze. "Did someone follow us?" she whispered.

"Impossible," said Caleb.

"Maybe someone beat us here?" asked Lexi.

"Maybe it's whoever is after me!" whispered Chase.

"Oh no," said Maddie. *Could it be Killian and Grace? They won't show us any mercy after we beat them last time.*

Two figures bounded down the passage, and Maddie and the others crouched down behind the Future Predictor. Maddie peered around the metal drum at a man and a woman in matching white tracksuits. The way they stood as they scanned the room for intruders made Maddie's heart squeeze painfully in her chest. They looked a little older, and they had obviously been cutting each other's hair, but she'd recognize them anywhere: it was HER PARENTS!!

"The rogue agents!" Caleb cried. "They've got the Illuminati symbol on their tracksuits!"

Maddie's heart leaped, and she started to run toward them. But then she stopped. They'd gone rogue, after all. She stood there, frozen to the spot, her mind racing with a thousand thoughts all at once. She couldn't believe her mom and dad were standing right in front of her. She'd longed for this moment every single day the last three years. She'd hoped and prayed that they were out there somewhere . . . and yet. Seeing them here confirmed something she'd been fearing ever since she and the other agents talked to Volkov. Her *parents* were villains. They'd been after Chase and the Future Predictor all along. And they'd found it. The only thing that Maddie couldn't figure out was *why*.

Maddie's mom reached out for her as Maddie blinked back tears.

"Don't come any closer!" Maddie said, more strongly than she felt.

"Maddie, it's us!" her dad said. "You remember your parents, right?"

Lexi smiled while Caleb, Doug, and Chase turned and stared openmouthed at Maddie.

"How can I trust you?" Maddie said, a lump in her throat. "You betrayed the Illuminati. And you abandoned me—for years! And now, now, you're . . . you're . . . *villains?*"

Doug gasped.

Lexi looked at Maddie warily. Maddie knew she need only give the word and Lexi would put her martial arts training to use.

"It's not what you think, honey," Maddie's mom said. "Let us explain."

"It's a long story," Maddie's dad said.

"But first, you need to know, we're Illuminati, but we're *not* villains," said Maddie's mom. "Three years ago, we followed the clues from Westminster Abbey and ended up here, at the North Pole."

"We only left once, to replant da Vinci's clues," said Maddie's dad.

"So you could find us," her mom explained.

"The scientific exploration was just a cover story," Maddie's dad explained. "We're both career Illuminati. Met at Camp Minerva back in training. It was love at first sight. You should've seen your mother deactivate a nuclear bomb underwater, surrounded by piranhas." He gave a low whistle.

"Dad! Irrelevant! How can I trust that you're telling the truth? Why were you guys gone so long? And why did you let me think you were . . . dead?" Maddie choked on the last word, remembering the pain and loss of the past three years, believing that she was an orphan.

"Oh, Maddie," Maddie's mom said. "It was the hardest thing we've ever done."

"Harder than capturing that giant squid in '98," Maddie's dad added. "And much harder than the time we averted that huge asteroid—"

"What!" Doug yelled. "What asteroid?!"

"Never mind, hon," Maddie's mom said. "It was terrible having to 'disappear' for so long without being able to tell you the truth. But the reason we were able to go through with it was because of this." She gestured to the Future Predictor.

"Because you believed in the mission? A cause greater than yourself?" Maddie asked.

"No, sweetie, because this machine told us that we would see you again. We used it to predict various outcomes, and it revealed that the only way this device would not fall into the wrong hands was if we stayed and guarded it—until the day you'd find us."

Maddie shook her head, trying to understand. "So . . . you knew I'd find you?"

"Yes," said Maddie's dad. "But that's as much as we could get out of it, so we've waited here, and you're right on time."

"You used your best muscle!" her mom said. "We knew you'd figure it out!"

Maddie remembered the message written in English

in the notebook they'd found at Westminster Abbey. Of course that phrase was familiar! It was all starting to make sense. Her parents had left it as a sign, just for her. So if her parents weren't villains . . . that meant she wasn't going to have to defeat them. Could it be that she actually . . . had them back? For real? She released the breath she'd been holding and began to laugh uncontrollably.

She ran headlong into them, nearly tackling them to the ground. She held on with both arms as the tears came fast and hot, and she buried her face in her parents' shoulders.

"Maddie!" her mom whispered, now crying, hugging Maddie so tight she thought she might pop.

"My little genius!" her dad said to the top of Maddie's

head, which was now damp from all her parents' tears. Maddie's mom untangled her arms from the hug briefly enough to salute Maddie's teammates, making a triangle with her hands.

The super spies returned the salute, and everyone took

a seat on the springy white floor. Maddie's mom and dad took turns explaining what had happened.

"We don't have a lot of luxuries here," Maddie's mom said. "But we've got enough hot chocolate for everyone! Now that we're reunited, it's time to celebrate! But first tell us, who are your friends?"

"This is my . . . team. This is Lexi, Caleb, Doug, and Chase. Everyone, these are my parents," Maddie said, trying to wipe the tears and snot from her face and not succeeding.

Just then, a loud beeping noise pierced the air. Everyone looked around to see where it was coming from. Doug covered his ears.

"What is that?" asked Maddie's dad.

"Did we set off an alarm when we came in?" asked Maddie.

"Yes, but this isn't it," said Maddie's mom, nearly shouting over the beeping, which was growing louder and louder.

"Guys . . . ," said Lexi. She pointed to Chase.

"Oh . . . my . . . ," said Caleb.

Maddie looked over at the pop star who'd become a close friend during their time together. She gasped.

The sound seemed to be coming from . . . Chase?

CHAPTER 25

Ride bene chi ride ultimo.
He who laughs best, laughs last.

Chase's eyes spun in their sockets like pinwheels, and his mouth opened unnaturally wide. The beeping continued to get louder, blaring like some sort of beacon.

"What is going ON?" Lexi screamed as Chase's head began to spin around and around on his neck. Doug fainted in Lexi's arms.

"He must not be human!" Caleb shouted. "Some kind of robot!"

Chase let out a long string of numbers. "That's our latitude and longitude!" said Maddie. She exchanged worried looks with her parents. This Chase-shaped robot was clearly alerting someone to their location.

Maddie covered her ears. She looked at Chase in horror.
"This whole time, Chase has been a robot?!" she said.

"But he's so lifelike!" said Lexi. "He looks like a person—"

"He talks like a person!" said Doug. "He even sings like a person!"

"Well, his dancing was always a little too good to be believed," said Caleb.

He fooled all of us, thought Maddie. *And millions of fans around the world.*

Just then, the automatic doors slid open with a whoosh, and a man zoomed through the opening. He hovered above the humans and Chase, held aloft by his rocket-powered boots. Maddie knew those boots—and she knew that face. Even though his goatee was gone, replaced by a silver mustache-and-soul-patch combo, she recognized him.

"I don't believe it," said Caleb.

"It's—" said Lexi.

"Zander Lyon," Maddie said with a sneer.

The Zander Lyon, the evil mastermind behind a plot

to steal all the world's energy, the former beloved inventor and CEO, famed adventurer and best-selling author, who'd betrayed the Illuminati when he decided to become a supervillain.

The same Zander Lyon who Maddie had caused to shoot sky-high and then land in the Hudson River, after he'd attacked her. He'd disappeared without a trace. Maddie—and everyone else—assumed he was gone for good.

"I'm ba-aack!" Zander trilled cheerfully. "It's been such a growth experience for me, let me tell you. I just needed some time away to properly plan for world domination once and for all!"

"You monster!" said Lexi.

"You maniac!" said Caleb.

"You . . . motorcycle!" said Doug. "Sorry, everyone was doing *M* words, I got confused."

"How are you still alive?" asked Maddie, confounded.

"Well, after our little . . . incident . . . I was rescued by a *lovely* elderly couple who had taken their sailboat for a spin. They saw me drowning and pulled me into their boat. Once we got ashore, I managed to hitch a ride to one of my super secret safehouses to regroup. I did a little yoga, drank a little green juice—"

"Yuck," said Doug.

"And got to work plotting how I'd get revenge on you pip-squeaks and take over the world once and for all," Zander said, with a self-satisfied megawatt smile.

"Didn't you learn your lesson about messing with the Illuminati last time?" Maddie said, anger in her voice.

"Don't you dare try anything," Lexi said, crouching into a fighting stance.

"And stay away from these children!" Maddie's mom shouted, in her *I'm only going to say this once* voice.

"So cute," Zander said, smiling evilly. "Chase! Stop that!"

Chase stopped beeping, and his head spun slower and slower until it came to a stop, unfortunately pointing backward. "Fix your head," he ordered. Chase's head rotated to the front. His eyeballs had stopped spinning, too, but they had turned a bright, glowing red.

"Chase is YOUR machine?" Maddie gasped.

Zander smiled proudly. "All mine. With a little help in the artificial voice department from certain megacorporations and cell phone companies. That's why his speech patterns are so realistic."

"Well, he says the word 'chill' far too much," Caleb pointed out.

"Silence!" Zander brought himself to the floor with a hiss of his Rocket Boots. "Chase, could you do the honors, please?" Chase stepped in front of the group. He turned his head toward the kids and offered a pained smile. "Sorry, fam," he said, and glowing red lasers burst from his eye sockets, creating a web that trapped Maddie, her parents, Caleb, Lexi, and Doug against one section of the rounded wall of the lair. Maddie took a pencil from behind her ear and poked it into one of the beams. It sizzled, and the smell of burnt wood filled the air as half the pencil disappeared into a cloud of ash. "Okay, then," she said.

"Chase! I thought you were our friend!" yelled Doug, tears welling in his eyes. "This is so not chill!"

Chase shrugged and gestured to Zander. "It's my programming," he said. "We had some good times, but I have to obey the Big Z."

Zander chuckled and whirled on his boots and strode over to the Future Predictor. He studied it awhile, then began to peer at the dials and gear settings. He made a few adjustments and cranked the handle. The cylinder started to spin, faster and faster, as the metal spirals pirouetted beneath it.

"First, I'll ask the machine how I'll take over the world," said Zander. "Then, if there's any time before dinner, I'll ask it what's the most painful way to dispose of Maddie and her little goon squad."

Maddie gritted her teeth. Zander saw her and smirked. "Oh, Maddie, I recognize that look. You would love to fight back, wouldn't you? But just so you understand how utterly defeated you are, let's ask the Future Predictor." Zander leaned down and spoke into one of the machine's metal cones. "Can Maddie Robinson escape? Can she somehow beat me again? Can she possibly hope to match my genius?" he said, practically cackling.

Slowly, a roll of parchment inside the machine rotated

as a metal arm controlled the scribbling of a quill pen. Zander read the parchment to himself and squealed with delight. He held it up for Maddie to see as he read it aloud:

"'Maddie Robinson will never be your equal.'"

Maddie's stomach dropped. She looked in horror at her parents, and then at her fellow super spies. The Future Predictor predicted that they would . . . fail? After all they'd gone through to track it down? She'd done more than she ever imagined—she'd found her parents. They'd captured Zander Lyon! She'd jumped off a château in ancient human wings, for Pete's sake!

"Here's one of my favorite Zanecdotes," said Zander, referencing his book of inspirational sayings. "The world was built by men like me—and it was built *for* men like me. I'll always come out ahead."

"That's not even what an anecdote is!" Maddie shouted, wishing she had a more clever response, or even better, a way to escape from Zander's trap.

Zander turned his attention back to the Future Predictor. He continued to play with the dials, whispering into the machine, turning the crank again, and jotting things down into his wrist-mounted holographic computer.

Maddie squared her shoulders. Something niggled in her mind: that the Future Predictor had told her parents that she was their only hope; that they'd come this far, that Leonardo himself *believed* in her. After all, Leonardo had left that message on the compass for her to find. He knew that she would make the right choices. But how could she win when the future-prediction device now said that she couldn't beat Zander? She looked at their captor, Chase, and suddenly had . . . an idea.

"I don't see a way out of this cage," Maddie whispered to her team. "But if I can gain control of Chase, maybe I can use him to stop Zander." She pulled out her hyper-phone and opened her hacking app. She began accessing Chase's interior algorithms—and rewriting them.

"Ugh, I don't feel so good," said Chase, struggling to deal with the rapid updates Maddie was wirelessly making to his operating system.

Zander looked up from the Future Predictor and scowled at Maddie. He instantly knew what she was trying to do. After all, he was an inventor himself.

"How dare you?" he shouted as he began typing into his wrist computer, trying to regain control of his robotic creation. "You think you can outsmart me? I'm your hero! Remember? I saw your potential when you were just a charity case at a stupid science fair! I told Archibald Archibald to recruit you!"

Maddie's cheeks flamed. Was it really he who had helped her get into the Illuminati and not her own merits? She paused in her coding for a split second as she wondered whether she'd have been smart enough, good enough, to get recruited on her own.

"He's lying!" Caleb yelled.

"Yeah, his name even sounds like 'lying'!" Lexi added.

"You can do this!" said Doug.

With her friends' encouragement, Maddie got back to reprogramming Chase, but she knew she was in trouble. She was a world-class coder, but Zander had literally written the coding language they were battling in. From her programming app, she could tell Zander was still in control of 70 percent of Chase's systems—and he was getting closer to full control with each passing second.

"Chase was my masterpiece!" Zander went on. "He fooled the world—even the Illuminati! No one ever suspected, not even the time he accidentally short-circuited during a Super Bowl performance. My AI tech is *that* good."

Keep him talking, Maddie thought. *I need more time to change Chase's programming.* "So you planned the whole thing?" she asked.

"Exactly! I embedded Chase in the Superstar Division, arranged for all those 'accidents' to happen on his tour, knowing that Volkov would assign you to guard him," Zander said with a smug grin, extremely impressed with his own machinations. "I saw everything through Chase's eyes—every step of your search for the Future Predictor. You idiots led me right to it!"

As Maddie and Zander battled for control of Chase's brain and body, Chase's laser eyes faltered and he fell to one knee. Zander entered a line of code, and Chase's left fist took a hard swing for the right side of his face. Just before impact, Maddie updated her code and Chase deflected his own punch. As Maddie and Zander traded lines of programming, Chase continued to fight himself, kicking himself in the shins and flipping himself over by the shirt collar.

Zander reached 80 percent control of Chase's operating system and the singer stood up ramrod straight. He formed another laser cage with his eyes and began creeping toward Maddie, the lasers getting closer and closer to burning her and her friends to a crisp.

"I could code before I could talk!" Zander shouted at Maddie. "You can't control Chase!" Zander was nearing 90 percent control of Chase, who was close enough to incinerate the super spies with a glance in any direction.

Zander's right, thought Maddie. *I can't control Chase. But maybe I'm not supposed to.* She thought back to the Chow Hall on Camp Minerva, where she'd reprogrammed the TuxBots. She immediately deleted her last hundred lines of code, even as Zander's control of Chase crept up to 95 percent.

Maddie was typing as quickly as she could, but she couldn't stop Zander from reaching 100 percent control of Chase. "Yes!" cried the deranged egomaniac who had once been Maddie's hero. "Chase, kill them!" he yelled. Instead, Chase hesitated. "This is a direct order!" shouted Zander. "Kill Maddie now!"

But Maddie wasn't worried. She continued typing determinedly into her coding app.

"I don't understand!" said Zander. "Why won't he obey me? I'm at a hundred percent control of him!"

Maddie calmly entered a final few keystrokes into her phone. "You forgot," she said, eyeing Zander, "Chase goes to one hundred and ten percent."

With a press of the enter key, Maddie uploaded her code into Chase—who turned off his laser eyes and fell to his knees as a surge of newfound power overloaded his operating system.

"Oooooh, baby, I'm feeling good," Chase crooned. He looked down at his hands as if he'd never seen them before. He jumped back to his feet. "Why do I feel so light all of a sudden?"

"That's because, for the first time, no one is controlling you," said Maddie. "Not Zander, not me, not even your assistant's assistant's assistant."

"I'm . . . free?" asked Chase.

"Yep," Maddie said. "I erased your old programming and replaced it with something more modern. Now you've got free will, just like us."

She gulped. "But that means you have to choose," she said, gesturing to Zander. "He's still trying to kill us. Will you save us? Or will you save Zander?"

Zander stepped forward, opening his arms wide, inviting Chase in for a hug. "My boy!" said Zander. "I was just about to give you free will myself, I swear. Now let's be clear: You can side with these losers against your own creator. Or you can join me. We can get rid of these annoying so-called 'do-gooders' and we can rule the world!" Chase rubbed his temples in thought. Zander continued, "We could make everyone in the world to listen to your music! Wouldn't you like that . . . son?"

Chase turned to Maddie with icy determination in his eyes.

It's all over, she thought. They were about to be defeated once and for all. Maddie took her mom's and dad's hands in her own and squeezed. At least they were together again. That made it worth it.

But in an instant, Chase's cold glare turned into the megawatt smile that had launched a million adoring lip-sync videos.

"Sorry, Big Z," said Chase. "I don't want to rule the world, I just want to make people dance! And one day, I'd like to fill up a tub with sparkling apple juice and take a bath in it. But mostly, I'd like to make people dance!" He pointed at Doug, who did his best impression of Chase's moves.

Chase turned his gaze to Zander. "Forcing people to do what you want them to do, that's so un-chill."

"You ungrateful robo-brat!" shouted Zander as he fired up his Rocket Boots, leaping into the air. Without hesitation, Chase fired a laser cage from his eyes, trapping

Zander against the wall of the Arctic base.

"I've sent our location to Illuminati HQ," said Chase. "According to my internal sensors, dozens of Illuminati agents will be here in less than one minute to apprehend Mr. Lyon. Maddie, I think you and your team can finally relax. I've got this, fam."

"This is impossible!" muttered the still-caged and still-dazed Zander. "How could she defeat me?" He yelled to Maddie, "The Future Predictor said you'd never be my equal!"

Maddie walked over to her onetime mentor. "I have my friends, who believe in me and help me. That's why I'll never be your equal. None of us will," she explained. "We'll be better."

Zander slumped down on the floor of his laser cage, a look of total shock and defeat on his face. Even his mustache drooped.

Maddie looked at Zander, then back to her friends and family, proud of everything she'd accomplished. "Not bad for a charity case, right?"

CHAPTER 26

Chi non fa, non falla is.

He who does nothing makes no mistakes.

A distant humming filled the air, and soon a fleet of flying minivans hovered outside the lair, surrounding it. The automatic doors opened, and a bright red flying minivan swooped in, carrying Volkov and a team of uniformed adult Illuminati agents. Sefu followed, hopping out of a light blue minivan.

"Maddie! Lexi! Caleb! Doug!" Sefu shouted. "I'm so glad you're okay!"

Volkov stepped purposefully out of the minivan, her jeweled eye glinting with steely determination, and her mouth pursed into an expression of pure disgust. "Zander Lyon, you are hereby officially arrested under the power of the All-Seeing Eye. You will be judged and imprisoned for your crimes."

She motioned for Chase to disable the laser cage he was keeping Zander in. She threw high-tech cuffs over Zander's wrists and gestured to the guards. "Load him into the red minivan."

Zander glowered at Maddie as the minivan doors closed. "This is not the last you'll see of me, little girl!"

Volkov looked at Maddie's parents. "I see going rogue runs in this family," she said. She made another quick gesture and several agents picked up the Future Predictor and loaded it into a flying minivan.

"What will you do with the machine?" asked Maddie.

"We will keep it safe at Camp Minerva," said Volkov. "We will attempt to uncover its secrets. However, you have proven the machine's flaw. But you knew that already, didn't you?"

"What flaw?" asked Caleb.

"The machine can only tell you so much," explained Maddie, picking up the piece of parchment that had predicted that she would never be Zander's equal. "Remember how da Vinci wrote about the pros and cons of creating the Future Predictor? 'Is the future stable? Or is it forever in flux?'"

"I remember," said Lexi.

"The reason da Vinci hid the machine was because its predictions would only be accurate at the moment they were made. But the future isn't stable—it can change."

"And you think we changed it?" asked Doug.

"Definitely," said Maddie. "You make your own future."

Volkov's serious expression turned into a smile. For an instant.

"Now *that's* using your best muscle!" Maddie's dad said.

"I'm so proud of you. But I'm just glad that we're finally reunited," her mom said, pulling Maddie into her ninety-ninth hug of the day.

"Those were the hardest years of our lives," her dad added, joining the hug and holding Maddie and her mom tight. "The only thing that kept us sane was knowing that someday you'd find us . . . and save the world!"

"And this isn't even the first time!" Doug piped up.

Maddie's heart swelled with so many emotions that she thought it might burst. The roller-coaster ride of seeing her parents again, learning that they'd gone rogue, and then realizing that they were the good guys after all made her head spin. Not to mention their friend Chase being a robot spy, and Zander Lyon reappearing—and almost taking over the world . . . again.

She embraced her mom and dad even tighter, which turned into a group hug when Doug leaped onto Mr. Robinson's back. Even Chase came in for a squeeze. Maddie wiped a tear from her eye. "Please don't disappear on me again," she whispered.

"We won't," said Mr. Robinson.

"That's a promise," added Mrs. Robinson. "I think we all have a lot to catch up on."

CHAPTER 27

Mangia bene, ridi spesso, ama molto.
Eat well, laugh often, love much.

A few weeks later, the backyard barbecue was in full swing at a two-story brick house on a tree-lined street in Center City, Philadelphia. The smell of hot dogs and hamburgers wafted over Maddie and her parents, who had just finished up on the grill. Now that Maddie's parents had returned, they'd bought back their old house and moved back in. Maddie had said a grateful goodbye to her cousins Jessica and Jay, and to the apartment where she'd lived the past couple of years. Their cat seemed glad to see Maddie—and her often loud, messy experiments—go. But Jessica, through tears, made Maddie promise to come visit soon.

Back at home, she'd moved into her old room—right

down the hall from her parents. But not everything was exactly the same. The Illuminati had helped them set up an amazing lab in the basement, hidden in a secret level beneath their regular basement, so that she could work on her inventions and do top secret Illuminati research without their neighbors suspecting a thing.

But being a family of super spies didn't come without a few secrets. Her parents got new business cards and called themselves "consultants" as a cover for their own top secret Illuminati work. Although they couldn't share the specific details of their new missions with Maddie, at the dinner table they talked about everything else, from Maddie's new inventions to the new bike lanes being built in their neighborhood. But sometimes, they talked about the best way to *hypothetically* protect the planet from solar flares, or high-tech methods to stop Venice from flooding due to climate change.

And the best part was, since her parents were Illuminati, she could actually have her Illuminati friends over. They even threw a big barbecue before the fall weather got too chilly. Maddie invited all her friends—using a letter written in Caleb's favorite code, the Vigenère cipher. The backyard felt as full as her heart. Everyone she cared about was here. Maddie's friends kept up the cover story for Jessica and Jay that they had met at summer camp last year. Which was true . . . technically. They just didn't mention the part about it being a camp for super spies.

Jessica and Jay chatted with Maddie's parents in the shade of a giant oak tree. Jay had brought a housewarming gift: a new microwave.

"I won a bunch of these in a contest," Jay said, referencing the time the Illuminati sent him fifty microwaves to replace the one Maddie had blown up. "I was keeping a couple for myself in case Maddie decided to take mine apart again, but I guess I don't have to worry about that anymore." Jay gave Maddie a loving fist bump.

"Maddie," said Jessica, "I almost forgot to ask: Did you see any whales on your trip?"

Maddie giggled. "Actually . . . I did," she said with a laugh. "Thanks for always being so understanding." She gave her cousin a huge hug for the years Jessica had spent looking after her.

Lexi, Caleb, Doug, and Sefu crowded around a huge picnic table laden with hot dogs, hamburgers, buns, toppings, macaroni salad, potato salad, cucumber salad, regular salad, cookies, cake, brownies, root beer, pickles, and lemonade.

"This is even better than Chase's party!" said Doug.

Lexi piled a plate high with cucumber salad and pickles, as well as a few brownies. Doug covered his plate in hot dogs with puddles of ketchup and mustard, and Caleb and Sefu had a bit of everything. Without their Illuminati jumpsuits, earpieces, and fanny packs full of gear, they looked just like regular kids. But Maddie knew the truth—they were

an elite team of highly trained, super secret super spies, who had just traveled the globe to unlock hidden mysteries, and saved the world . . . again.

Maddie slipped her hand into her pocket and fiddled with the compass that Leonardo had left for her. She often twirled it around in her fingers, as a reminder that no matter what anyone told her, she could decide her own future.

She knew that soon, flying minivans would arrive to invisibly whisk her fellow super spies home. After all, they had families of their own and the rest of the school year to catch up on. And Maddie would go back to school on Monday. But she knew this year would be different. Yes, she'd miss her friends, and yes, she'd still have to keep it a secret that she'd saved the world another time. But her parents were back. She walked over to them, and they wrapped her in a big family hug.

"I love you," Maddie said to them both.

"We love you too," her mom said as she kissed the top of Maddie's head.

All was right again in the world.

CHAPTER 28

La calma è la virtù dei forti.

Calm is the virtue of the strong.

A few weeks later

Back at school, it was time for Maddie's history presentation on Leonardo da Vinci, before the end of the semester and holiday break. Mr. Onderdonk was dressed like the painter, including the floppy hat, and introduced each student before they spoke. Maddie's palms were sweating, and she felt butterflies in her stomach. The whole school was watching these presentations, and she'd never spoken in front of a crowd this big before.

When it was finally Maddie's turn, she reached into her pocket and gripped the compass that da Vinci had given her. "Wish me luck, Leonardo!" she whispered.

She unveiled her project and climbed aboard. Inspired by da Vinci, Maddie had built one of his prototypes with historically authentic materials. It was a mechanical lion, made of metal, which had taken her several weeks to get right in her basement lab. She rode the lion across the stage and waved. The other students gasped and cheered. The lion stopped in the center of the stage and opened its jaws, and a bouquet of flowers popped out from its mechanical mouth. Mr. Onderdonk's jaw dropped open.

Maddie launched into her presentation. "This mechanical lion," she said, "shows how perfectly da Vinci blended known science and innovation. It takes inspiration from the world of nature, but da Vinci combined it with cutting-edge physics and mechanics."

Maddie compared the lion to some of da Vinci's more practical, better-known inventions and their modern-day counterparts. "Da Vinci's diving mask is like a submarine built for one. His flying machines are like airplanes from another dimension. And his idea for a parachute . . . well, that was a lot like a regular parachute. But he came up with it five hundred years ago!"

Maddie paused to catch her breath, hopping down from the metal lion. It wasn't super comfortable to ride on, after all. *I should've added a saddle*, she thought. As she neared the end of her speech, the entire auditorium was silent. Everyone was captivated by her presentation—even Johnny hadn't interrupted with a burp.

"Da Vinci was ahead of his time," she said, "and his ideas would change the world. But thousands of pages of his work are missing. Who knows what other brilliant inventions have been lost?"

As the whole school applauded, Maddie smiled to herself, because only she knew the answer. She saw Mr. Onderdonk clapping backstage, and the principal of the school was smiling in the front row. Seated next to the principal was a man with a stern face and kind eyes—or maybe it was a kind face with stern eyes. He made eye contact with Maddie—and winked. Just then, Maddie's S.M.A.R.T.W.A.T.C.H. buzzed:

REPORT TO HQ. YOUR NEXT MISSION IS ABOUT TO BEGIN.

EPILOGUE

A straight-backed boy clicked officiously down the long, dim hallway, several stories underground. The walls were tall and made of an impenetrable steel, and the air was slightly dank. Fluorescent lights flickered above the boy at intervals, illuminating his blond pompadour and the array of medals pinned to his chest.

He reached a transparent cube at the end of the hallway, made of bullet- and shatterproof glass threaded with steel bars, with a few small breathing holes in the ceiling. A man sat cross-legged in the center of the cube. It was Zander Lyon, in an Illuminati-issued prisoner jumpsuit. His silver beard and hair had grown long, and he appeared to be meditating.

The boy cleared his throat. Zander opened his eyes. "Nice to see you, Killian," he said.

The boy looked around and behind him, then straightened his shoulders. He pulled out a tiny device from his pocket and pressed a button. Something clicked, and one wall of the cube swung outward, like a door opening. Killian gestured to the open door. Zander stepped out and took a deep breath.

"Young man," said Zander, "how would you like to destroy the Illuminati with me?"